I love the way this gorgeous meditation veers with daring and grace between poetry and prose, between art and life.

—Hilma Wolitzer

M.G. Stephens' *History of Theatre* or *the Glass of Fashion* is the seasoned work of a pure poet and fiction writer, a marriage of the concise and lyrical, suffused with both moments of keenly observed humanity and flights of luminous rumination.

—Richard Price, author of *The Wanderers* and *Lush Life*

The whole is funny, grave and grand. Simply terrific.

—George Szirtes, author of *Reel* and
The Burning of the Books

A totally captivating genre-bending set of monologues, well, no, let's say prose poems—well, let's say—what a voice!

—Miranda Beeson, author of *Catch & Release*

D1452099

Also by M. G. Stephens

FICTION
Season at Coole
The Brooklyn Book of the Dead
Shipping Out
Still Life
Circles End
Jigs and Reels
History of Theatre or the Glass of Fashion
King Ezra
Kid Coole

POETRY
Alcohol Poems
Paragraphs
Tangun Legend: Korean Bear Myth
After Asia
Translations (from Korean)
Occam's Razor
Top Boy
Resist (Political Poems)
Hobo Haiku

NONFICTION
Green Dreams: Essays under the Influence of the Irish
Where the Sky Ends
The Dramaturgy of Style
Lost in Seoul and Other Discoveries on the Korean Peninsula
Going Thoreau

PLAYS
Our Father
Horse
Adam's Curse
R & R
Walking Papers
Breezy Point
Cracow
Gypsies
Comrades
Maggie & Jinx

KING EZRA

M. G. Stephens

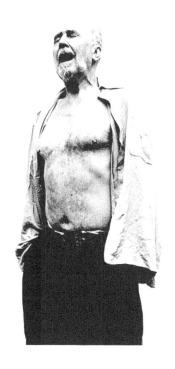

SPUYTEN DUYVIL
New York City

Library of Congress Cataloging-in-Publication Data

Names: Stephens, Michael Gregory, author.
Title: King Ezra / M.G. Stephens.
Description: New York City : Spuyten Duyvil, [2022] |
Identifiers: LCCN 2022003611 | ISBN 9781956005516 (paperback)
Subjects: LCGFT: Novels.
Classification: LCC PS3569.T3855 K56 2022 | DDC 813/.54--dc23
LC record available at https://lccn.loc.gov/2022003611

i.m.o.

Harold King

"What thou lovest well is thy true heritage
What thou love'st well shall not be reft from thee"

—EP, "Canto LXXXI"

PART ONE

THE DETENTION TRAINING CENTER (DTC)

PISA, ITALY

"[Only shadows enter my tent
As men pass between me and the sunset,]
beyond the eastern barbed wire
a sow with nine boneen
matronly as any duchess at Claridge's"

—"Canto LXXX"

Chapter One

"Will people accept them?
(i.e. these songs).
As a timour wench from a centaur
(or a centurion),
Already they flee, howling in terror."
—"Tenzone"

And he had gotten hold of a pair of hiking boots and put them on, and with a knapsack on his back, he lit out for the territory beyond the pale of the city. Rome is where he started, and he did manage to secure a ride on a train that got him to the outskirts of the city, finding transportation to Florence, then Bologna, and Milano, though in each leg of the journey, he also legged it. And from Milano he went to Lichstenstein, and walked to Gais, up up, into the Alps, up up into the snowy trails, his fearless boots on his feet, he trudged to Switzerland. And from there he boarded a bus and went even further, north and then northeast, west and then north and northeast again. From then on, he walked. Oh, he knew all about walking, and his age was no barrier. He had walked all over Provence when he was a young man; he certainly could walk from Rome into the Italian Alps, despite the distance from Rome. But the journey being improvised, full of spontaneity—read here stubborn indifference to the misery it might cause him or others—and he hoofed it, skipping along at times, belying his age, which was almost sixty, his clothes were raggedy, but then again everyone's clothes were that way. It was war, and

Italy was not doing well. The outcome looked questionable. The new government was set up in Salo, at the edge of Lago di Garda (Lake Garda). He had a map. But a map was not the territory, he thought. Once he began to walk, his feet hurt. It had been decided, he told himself, that he would visit his daughter Mary in Gais. A peasant family in the mountains had taken care of her since she was a baby. Now she was a young woman. He wondered how she was. That was the spur that prodded him onwards, to visit Mary at any cost. Who knew what the future held for someone like him? The Fascists were losing their asses to the Allies. There was so much to tell her, not just about the war and his radio broadcasts in Rome—the last one he would do having just been recorded—but about their lives. Poetry begins to atrophy when it goes too far from music, he thought. He wanted to instruct her about his own writings, but also about this complex family of whom Mary knew nothing. He had a wife named Dorothy; and she had a son named Omar. And then there was Olga, his mistress of many years, and Mary's mother. He needed to explain to Mary why her mother had sent her off to live among the peasants in the Alps. There were his *Cantos* to write, some of which having laid fallow in his brain for a decade or longer. There were the already published *Cantos* that he wanted-ed to explain to Mary what they were all about, not explain the bloody things, but to give a map as it were of its partic-ulars. *Mi faccia vedere su questa carta*, he thought. If only it were that easy. These things would be resolved now or they never would be resolved. Walking was good, he loved to walk, and he appreciated the vigorous life, and he had been nothing if not vigorous all of his own rich life, well, not so much rich in things as it was in people and places, in ideas, and most important of all, in words, literature, to be exact, poetry, in particular. Yeats, Possum and Wyndham, they had no ground beneath 'em. Jimmy Joyce was another matter entirely. His divine fire of genius was fueled by John Jameson's and Sons, water from the Liffey, mud and all. And when Ezra was a young man, he had walked all over Provence because he wanted to understand the troubadours, from the soles of his feet upwards through the torque of his body, the heart to the hand, from the brain to the heart, from the hand to the words upon the page. He had walked in the grooves set down by the troubadours, his own personal favorites. And now he walked as then and sang Provençal songs or recited poems by Guido (Cavalcanti) or Pere (Vidal), and whistled part of the "Four Seasons" by Vivaldi, whom he had helped to re-discover, and whom Olga had performed at her music festivals across Italy, back before there was a war, and Rapallo was home, peaceful and serene, sophisticated and civilized. And so he walked into the mountains, his legs aching, and there were blisters on his feet, and because the roads were dusty and potted and gutted, he began to look like a tramp, which he did not mind. He pictured himself a kind of Italian Basho, wending through the narrow north, searching for enlightenment. And he thought about Confucius' *Analects*, and how he might journey to Salo after seeing Mary to put Benito Mussolini straight about Kung's great wisdom. He needed to educate the Duece, as he called him, about Jefferson and Confucius. A simple task, that. But night was coming on. The sun had gone down from the blazing sky. Night seeped into his field of vision, and he knocked on the door of some rural folk, asking for a place to lodge, for some food, now looking a bit like a mendicant. He laughed, thinking: maybe I have turned into Tolstoy in my old age, moving about the countryside like a mad monk and not a bona fide leopard of a poet, the poet-king, Yeats and Joyce used to call it, telling him, when they were in good moods, Joyce in his cups, Yeats off with the fairies, they would speak to him of the Irish poet-kings. Perhaps the Italian hill peasants thought he was a bit like St. Francis of Assisi, whose poetry he had translated and whose wildness he appreciated more than the saint's holiness. Brother Sun and Sister Moon. Or was it the reverse, Sister Sun, Brother Moon. No, no, hang it all, Robert Browning, there could be but one Ezra Pound, and this Ezra Pound. The hill peasants gave him a simple fare: a bowl of bean soup (*fagioli*), a piece of stale bread, a half glass of red wine, and he fell asleep in the chair, waking in the morning before they got up and he went off out the door, singing a song that James Joyce had once sang, though he couldn't for the life of him remember all the words, so he simply hummed it, walking and walking, until he felt as if he might collapse, and eventually came upon another mountain village of only a few stalwart buildings, far from the ruins and chaos of war, they welcomed him in, and listened in amusement to this crazy American's Italian stories, the accent all wrong, though his vocabulary was vast, and his grammar was *perfetto*, a bit stiff but right on the lira. What thou lovest well remains, he thought. *EP exults in the extra inch wherever the 'ell it's found, but wasn't JJ a son of a binch to send him an extra pound?* Ah, but the rest is dross, he thought, accepting the simple fare that the hill people, most of them hill widows, absent their hill bachelors, offered him. By early afternoon, he progressed further towards Gais and Mary. By nightfall on the second day, he rested outside a shuttered inn, hoping to find someone to give him some food and a place to sleep, only no one appeared, the village was empty. The hill bachelors were gone, and so were the hill widows. Even the hill children were gone, but an echo of their once laughter still rang in the valley. Everyone had gone away. War was like that. They may have fled to a safer place only to be killed there or they may have fled in a panic or fled because they were Jews and the Jews were being rounded up, even in Italy, and sent off to the concentration camps, if you believed that malarkey that the propagandists were spewing. The Jews were fine and they could always take good care of themselves. No one had to worry about them, he thought, though he was often wrong about so many things these days. There was not a soul to be found, so he fell asleep, hungry, sitting in front of the closed inn. In the morning, he walked, the blisters worse than ever, now infected and making him walk haltingly, in great pain. He was filthy, a dustball from head to toe. The stinking hiking boots were worthless, but he could not walk without them, so he trudged onwards into the afternoon when he eventually found another village higher up in the mountains, and this one had people who welcomed him and gave him some food and let him sleep for a few hours, resting his head on the wooden table of the inn. They used herbs to rub on his blistery feet to soothe and heal his perambulatory wounds. Their ministrations were so good, he decided to keep walking deeper into and up the mountains. He walked, this time, through the night, animal eyes looking at him, tripping and stumbling, he heard growls and howls, rumblings in the underbrush, and he shivered from the cold and shivered from the fear that possessed his otherwise indomitable spirit. As he walked these words entered his mind, almost like a poem coming to mind for the first time, though almost immediately, he knew better: *Dawn, to our waking, drifts in the green cool light.* Who had written those lines? he asked himself. Was it Yeats or maybe even Joyce or Eliot? Did Wyndham Lewis write them, No, he said aloud, why not, he was walking alone, no, it was I, he said. It was I who wrote those lines. "Canto IV." They lay at the commencement of *The Cantos*. But its beginnings were so many years ago, he found himself fumbling to remember how the line came into being, and he came up empty. That was what happened to the mind; it had ways of tricking you into believing things that were not true, and to dismiss other things that were true.

Finally he arrived in Gais, but when he presented himself in the courtyard in front of the house where Mary lived, she did not know who he was or what he was doing there.

Mary was working in the garden.

When she heard someone coming up the path that led to

the cottage where she lived with the two farmers her mother had taken her to many years earlier, she said:

—Who's there?

Her father, her 60-year-old father came around the bend, but she did not recognize him. She thought he was a tramp, looking to cadge a meal from her.

She repeated her question.

—Who's there?

—Hamlet's ghost! he shouted.

Once he opened his mouth, she realized it was her father, Ezra Pound.

—Babbo! Mary cried.

—*Oh, figlia! Mia figlia*!

Ophelia, he thought. He must remember to write it down. *Ophelia*. Figlia. Oh, figlia! Why had he not realized that a long time ago. *Hamlet* was about, as Confucius called them, right relations. Father to son, daughter to father. Mother to child. Husband to wife; wife to husband. Et cetera, etc.

His feet were sore and blistered quite badly. How many miles had he walked? He had journeyed more than 800 kilometers from Rome, but how much of that journey had he walked? Maybe half of it; maybe more. He had been walking for days. He was covered in dust from head to foot, he wore enormous hiking boots and had on hiking clothes.

—How did you get here, Babbo?

—I walked from Rome, Pound said.

—How did you walk from Rome, Babbo?

Mary thought that her father was teasing.

You could hear the skepticism in her voice, as if her pranking father was rendering yet another prank upon her.

—How did I get here from Rome? he asked. One step at a time, he said, laughing, even though his feet bled and his legs felt like lead and his clothes smelled as though he were dead.

—Are you all right? Mary asked her father.

—I never thought that a poet would detest feet so much, he said, nodding towards his stinking feet.

He sat on a wooden crate and untied his laces and painfully removed the oversized hiking boots from his blistery feet. Bloody hell, he said, trying to sound like his friend James Joyce, with a slight Dublinesque brogue. But he only sounded like that suburban American rube Ezra Pound, doing panto.

—Your feet are terribly blistered, Mary said, examining the bloody stumps.

She ran inside and came quickly back with medication and bandages and gauze, scissors to cut the bandages. As she attended to his medical needs, she asked why he was there. What had brought him up into the mountains?

—I am wanted, he declared. Dead or alive.

Again Mary thought he was kidding.

—I am so glad to see you. You are always wanted here, Babbo.

—No, he said, I really am wanted for treason, by the United States of Amirka, 'cause of my broadcasts on Rome radio. Can you imagine, Mary?

His broadcasts were nearly incomprehensible. What could be treasonous about a poet's sound-bites, his crazy rhythms, and his word-obsessions?

Out of nowhere, Pound said: Mary, Mary, quite…

—I love when you say that, Babbo.

Mary paused and thought.

—They are foolish if they believe that is treason.

In the interim as he rested his feet, she had gone inside and then came out with a plate of bread and cheese, slices of *soppressata* (salty and fatty and delicious), some fruit, olives, a glass of wine, even a few figs.

—It is beyond foolish, my dear, he told her.

—I will hide you, Babbo.

—I can hide but I can't run.

—What will you do?

He was silent for a moment. Later he would become famously silent for long periods, days on end, months on end, even years. But here he was simply ruminating, looking for the words to express himself. Though a poet, he was notorious for lacking any ability to express his feelings beyond outrage and disgust. Injustice did not seem to offend him at all, nor prejudice, nor the misery of people during the war years. He had words, but he seemed to lack an emotional vocabulary to express what it was he was feeling, as though what he felt was not important compared to what he knew, what he had experienced, and who he had known and more important, what he had read. What he had read constituted his world, and his world was not insignificant, for he had been friends with practically everyone (everyone important to the arts, literary, musical and visual), especially many years ago, in London, in Paris, out in the world.

So he stumbled as he spoke to his daughter.

—I came to talk to you. There are many things you need to know. If I don't tell you now, you'll find out in the newspapers or on the radio. They will distort what is the truth.

Mary's Italian was impeccable, but her English was not.

She said: I need to hear it, as it were, from the mouth of the horse.

Pound smiled.

—Indeed, he said. The mouth of the horse. *In bocca dal lupo.*

In the mouth of the wolf, he thought. The wolf dies.

—Let me make you a cup of tea, Babbo.

—I'm all right. There is very little time.

Mary peeled off his filthy clothes and came back with a sponge and hot water and some soap. Where had she found the soap? he wondered. He thought of Tching who wrote on his bathtub: Make It New! Day by day, make it new. As if reading his mind, she said aloud: Make It New, and he laughed at his daughter's uncanny ability to comprehend him, even at this nonverbal level, mind to mind. They were in synch. They had always been that way. Even if he had not been there for her during most of her upbringing. When he was there, they connected marvelously.

—I am so glad to know you, she said.

—And there is so little time, he answered.

—Tell me, Papa.

He looked as if he might cry.

—It pains me to have to tell you these things.

He spoke of complications within complications within complications. Mary said that there were always complications within other complications. That is life, she said. It is a basic rule of drama. He laughed at that remark, even though his blistered feet were so painful, he thought he might cry in front of his own daughter. I am your father, he said. And I your filial daughter, she said.

He went on to tell her that there were others besides her mother Olga. Mary asked if he meant that he had a mistress.

—I mean that your mother is not my wife.

—You have a wife.

—In Rapallo. Her name is Dorothy. (He paused) Her name is Dorothy Shakespear.

—That's impressive, Mary said. You married Shakespeare's daughter.

They laughed.

The laughter cut the tension considerably.

—She is not Italian?

—No, she is not Italian.

She is British.

We married a long time ago.

We have a son.

MARY. A son?

EP. Yes.

MARY. I have a brother?

EP. Not exactly, darling dear.

MARY. I am lost, Babbo.

EP. Dorothy had an affair with an Egyptian.

MARY. And you had an affair with my mother Olga.

EP. I love your mother dearly.
I love you dearly.
You are my heart and soul.

MARY. So who is my pseudo-brother?

EP. His name is Omar.
He lives in England.
You are not related.
He is your stepbrother.
This is so complicated.
I am sorry, cara.
I am so sorry, dear Mary.

MARY. But you are really my father?

EP. Of course I am your father.

MARY. I just wanted to be sure.

He told her that whatever happened, he was her father. That is why he had walked from Rome to speak to her. Things were about to change, he knew, and she might not see him again for a long time.
—I am so pleased to see you.

MARY. The world is falling apart.
Like your friend Yeats wrote,
"the center does not hold,
Things fall apart…"

EP. I will be arrested soon.
They may execute me
For treason.

MARY. There is no reason
To do that, Babbo.

EP. I have tried to make it cohere.

MARY. And does it?

EP. If not the poem,
Then maybe the life,

It coheres.
We are together,
However briefly.

I have always loved you,
I will always love you.

MARY. And my mother?

EP. She is another matter,
Your mother.
She loves you in her way.

MARY. In her way?

He explained that Olga had rejected her as a baby because she was not a boy. He apologized for her mother's behavior. But he wanted her to know that Olga had changed. Now that she had gotten to know Mary, she loved her deeply.

—I am sorry to disappoint her.

But he was not sorry. He told her that love was the answer. All the rest is dross, he said. He emphasized that word "dross." Mary wanted to know if they were going to work on translations. Are you going to teach me how to read and understand your poem? By "poem" Mary meant *The Cantos*. Was her father going to give her a roadmap of its understanding?

EP. I will return.
Someday.
Soon.

MARY. Oh, Babbo.

EP. I never rejected you.

MARY. Even when you lived in Rapallo
And would come up into
The hills to visit me
And my mother
In Sant'Ambrogio?

EP. My love
Sempre

Always

Mary Mary quite…

Sempre
Sempre

CHAPTER TWO

"Nor can who has passed a month in the death cells
believe in capital punishment
No man who has passed a month in the death cells
believes in cages for beasts"
  —"Canto LXXXIII"

1.

The American military had set up the cages for high-value prisoners.

Ezra Pound was one of them: he looked more like a crazy artist, not a holy Fascist terror, the propaganda arm of Mussolini's drive through the heart and soul of Italy.

Pound paced the guerrilla cage, almost like a circus animal or some deranged character in a side show folly. It was six grim feet by six grim feet by six terrible feet. It was opened to the elements on all sides: mud on the ground, wind and dust from all sides, the sun beating down from the top. Ants. Scorpions. Bees. Rats scuttling by. Crows waiting to eat your carrion flesh. Ezra was nearly six grim feet tall, so he had to slouch in order to be inside the gorilla cage, as he called it. He was terrified; he had become terrified given the circumstances; the incarceration was wholly unexpected. He had gone to the Americans to help them, not to be arrested and locked up in a cage like a circus animal. He had a phobia about being caged. His anxieties had exploded. His brain did not work properly in these conditions.

American soldiers guarded the poet.

He had gone to the Americans naively thinking that he could offer them help in how they were going to rebuild Italy.

They seized him and brought him here to Pisa.

Soldiers walk past.

Some notice the old man, with his odd beard and funny clothes, in the cage. Others pass him by, without even seeing him. The war has done that to them. The war had hardened their muscles, and the heart is a muscle, and it has become hardened too. They have seen human skeletons moving around in the concentration camps. They have stepped over their comrades in war zones. The world can be an awful place. The idea of an American poet confined to a cage is not the worst thing these soldiers had seen.

—I used Jefferson as my guide, Pound says.

—I am not allowed to communicate with the enemy, sir.

It is the young soldier guarding the poet who says that. He refers to the poet as "the enemy." Have things come to that?

Pound offers him a bone:

—We are fellow Merkins, sirrah.

—Orders is orders.

—Orders am, Pound says, ever the poet.

—I'm just doing what I was told. That's the military.

—I always tried to do what I wasn't told, Pound said. There's the rub.

But the soldier wasn't even paying attention to his prisoner anymore. He asked who was there and when he did,

Pound thought of Hamlet and its opening. Who's there? He remembered visiting his daughter Mary in the northern mountains, and how she asked—who's there?—when he came upon the clearing where she stood in front of the house where she was raised and still lived. As if reading the poet's mind, the soldier said:

—Who's there?

—Your relief, another soldier said.

They were so young, these American soldiers, and Ole Ez felt so old, almost ancient, a kind of dinosaur. The soldier guarding Pound shouted, Announce yourself! as another soldier entered the area.

—Private Callahan, sir.

The first soldier's relief had arrived; now he could go back to his tent and relax a little bit before going to sleep. He explained to the new soldier the rules that needed to be followed with the poet Ezra Pound.

—We are not supposed to fraternize or even speak with this enemy combatant, the first soldier said.

Pound took umbrage with the descriptives.

—I am not an enemy combatant. I am an American poet, you yahoos. I'm suffering from hypertension, dehydration, starvation, vertigo, glaucoma, and claustrophobia.

The first soldier ignored the prisoner. He spoke to the relief on hand.

—Under no circumstances are we to engage him in conversation.

—Very good, sir.

The first soldier left the scene, leaving it to the new one.

—There's a perigee moon out tonight, Pound said, pointing upwards to the moon.

His head scraped the top of the gorilla cage, as he called it, and his right hand banged across the wire mesh of the "ceiling." The new soldier remained tight-lipped and did not respond to Ezra. By this point Pound was dirty and freakish in the cage, looking like something you might see in a flea-bag side-show at a carnival in the Midwest of America.

Pound pleaded with the guard.

—What have I done?

Suddenly the new soldier spoke.

—That question is beyond my remit, sir.

2.

Where is the poetry? And where does the poet belong? In the high Irish ancient world, the poet was king. Willie Yeats and Jimmy Joyce, they both talked about this. They often talked to Ezra about the poet-kings of Ireland. It was the tradition in that part of the world. Everything depended upon the bard. Poetry was built on the facts, and the facts led to the truth. The poet was the myth-maker and the sovereign of the tales, the artificer of the community and their known world. S/he was a singer and a scolder, a tolder and an unfolder; the skald was the poet in those times, maker of words, inventor of names for things, dictionary and thesaurus, source of great wonders. The last place you would put a poet is in a cage, even a poet whose politics were reprehensible, unforgiveable, disgraceful, aberrant, ugly, and wrong. You'd try to reason with him. He was not a danger to himself or others, face to face. It was his ideas—and his politics—that were so abominable. His ideas were on the wrong side of history, bigoted, narrow-minded, cruel, without compassion. That being said, where did Pound wind up? They put him in a cage, six feet by six feet by six feet, and he was just a little under six feet himself. They put him in a cage outside with the elements, the light in his eyes, the dust up his nose and down his throat and burning his eyes. Franco killed the poet Federico Garcia Lorca; the CIA and the Chilean military killed the poet Pablo Neruda. The U.S. tried to destroy Ezra Pound, killing him in that inhumane cage. They threw slops into his cage when they had to feed him. Soldiers were forbidden to talk to him. He was the enemy. He was a traitor, they said. He would be brought to book in the United States. They would process him at the Detention Training Center in Pisa, then fly him back for a trial, a trial about treason, and convict him; and then they would execute him or send him to prison for life. No one had thought the endgame through just yet. Capture him, lock him up, guard him like he was the most dangerous character on earth. He would piss and shit in front of the other prisoners and the guards. The other prisoners were murderers and out and out psychos, AWOL soldiers, soldiers who lost their courage or their will to live, broken men. One by one they were tried and executed. It was a bit like a meat market, an abattoir; people had gotten so used to killing one another. It was just part of being there.

You put them in cages, convicted them in a military court, executed them, took the body and threw it in a ditch. The problem with Ezra Pound was that he was not a military man, not a soldier; he didn't go AWOL from his post, didn't kill anyone on the base. They weren't really sure what to do with him. He lost weight; he complained of being fearful of this kind of confinement. He was claustrophobic. He was a free spirit. Crazy, yes, but brilliant, they said, all those books, all those languages he referenced, all that history, American and European, Chinese and Japanese that was regurgitated in those unreadable, incomprehensible poems, not to mention his reprehensible politics.

It was all moot.

He was in a cage.

Ole Ez wuz a criminal? Give me a fucking break, world! But there you have it, the great poet in a cage, held by the American military. The war had ended. Italy had lost, and one of the spoils of war was the head of Ezra Pound, if not on a stick, then in this outdoor cage. To the victors go the spoils, and the DTC was a spoil of that war. Italy was broken; Italy had lost the war. There were the broken pieces everywhere. People said it would be years before Italy was ever the same again. Maybe it would never recover. Don't worry. Ole Ez is going to make lemonade from these lemons he was given. He's going to write away in the gorilla cage, and it will come out as *The Pisan Cantos*, a truly great work of poetry, complex, multi-leveled, even a precursor of multimedia, a poem that was not just simply linear, but spatial, inhabiting a universe and on different planes; three dimensional, even.

3.

EP. We are two Americans, you and I.
When we bleed, we bleed American blood.
We are patriots.

SOLDIER 2. I understand that you are under arrest for treason.

EP. What is treason?

SOLDIER 2. I can't answer that question either.
But I do know this: it is punishable by death.

EP. Death?

SOLDIER 2. That's right—death.

EP. What have I done?

SOLDIER 2. That's for the generals and others to sort out.
That's up to God.

EP. God?

SOLDIER 2. God will help you if you pray to him.

EP. Dear Zeus, tell me what the feck is happening here.

SOLDIER 2. I meant praying to the true god, who is Jesus Christ.

EP. Christ all mighty!

SOLDIER 2. My job is to guard this cage.

EP. I have friends in high places.

SOLDIER 2. I can't comment on that, sir.

EP. I'm a poet.

SOLDIER 2. I have no doubt that justice will be served.

EP. Justice?

SOLDIER 2. To the victor go the spoils.

EP. I could clap my hands and this cage might disappear.

SOLDIER 2. I would advise you not to do that, sir.

EP. I could click my fingers and *voila*! There is no more gorilla cage.

4.

Pound snaps his fingers. Nothing. He does it again. Kung appears. You might know Kung by a different name, so I will give it to you here. Confucius. He was dressed in ancient Chinese court regalia. At the touch of Kung's hand, the gorilla cage falls away. Kung and Pound dance, a crazy kind of kabuki dance or maybe a dithyramb from ancient Greece, a kind of goat song, priapic and pagan. As old as he is, Pound does cartwheels across the floor, and Kung follows him. It is something you might not expect to happen between two such serious people. But there it is. They now dance almost like Irish dancers, tapping out a beat with the leather from their shoes. They sit down exhausted. Ezra says how good it is to see Kung and the old Chinese philosopher acknowledges his pupil, saying how good it is to see him. They have known each other a long time, it turns out. They have been in constant communication for many years. They know each other's ideas. There is a kind of respect that has grown up around them, Kung for Pound mostly, because in the reverse, Pound for Kung, that has always been a given in the poet's long complicated life. He and Kung are kindred spirits. They see the world and its order in similar ways.

—They don't understand.

—Who? Kung asks him.

—The world, Ezra answers.

—Why? Confucius inquires.

Pound smiles.

—Tching wrote it on his bathtub.

Kung smiles.

Pound now sang: Day by day. Make it new.

Confucius sits on a bed of pillows that seem to appear out of nowhere. He sits cross-legged and bids Ezra Pound to join him, which the poet does.

—Shall we go down to the river in a boat filled with other poets and civil servants?

Suddenly Pound looks ten years younger, all of his cares and worries dissolved.

—The usual suspects? he asks Confucius.

Even Kung knows what Ezra Pound's tastes are. Regarding the usual suspects, he says:

—Dante, Guido, Tu Fu, Li Po, Eliot…

—Eliot? Pound is not sure if he wants Eliot in this company.

—He is your friend? Kung asks.

—We are friends, yes. But Eliot is such a stick-in-the-mud.

—Then he shall not be in the poets' boat.

Pound claps his hands and dances a goatish dance, seeming not to believe that he is no longer in the gorilla cage.

EP. And Li Po made love
To the moon
In the river.

KUNG. And he drowned.

EP. Yes, he drowned.

KUNG. That is not going to happen to us, my friend, my dear Ezra.
You are safe with me.
All is well.
Shall we go?

EP. How?

KUNG. The way out is via the door.

EP. Why is it that no one will use this method?

KUNG. Tching wrote it on his bathtub.

EP. Make It New!

(Pound and Kung walk off together, arm in arm)

Chapter Three

"Hang it all, Robert Browning,
there can be but the one 'Sordello.'
But Sordello, and my Sordello?"
　—"Canto II"

In the autumn of 1966, having dropped out of a state university earlier in the year, Dermot Froidveaux had moved back to New York, found a job at the New York Public Library, and moved into a railroad apartment on East 10th Street between First and Second avenues, and that's when he began to call himself a poet. After all, he had published a few poems in various magazines, such as *The World*, *For Now*, and *Galley Sail Review*. He had a mustache and long curly hair, a pair of jeans which he constantly wore, along with a pair of suede pull-on work boots which he had purchased at Hudson's, a nearby Army & Navy store. He had found a nice corduroy jacket, along with a warm navy-colored pea coat that happened to still have a watch cap in one pocket. He wore work shirts and a battered old ties he found in another charity shop. He was not a beatnik, even though that is what some of his relatives called him when they saw how he had changed. He told them that he was not a beatnik, but a hippie. They did not know the term. He was twenty years old, a college dropout, and now living on East 10th Street between Second and First avenues in the East Village, the old Lower East Side. His family had disowned him, and he had disowned his family. He was a new person, the future, he said, a poet and a peacemaker, not a soldier, not a patriot. The future is right here before us on the Lower East Side. Like Thoreau, he was an agitator, a practitioner of civil disobedience. He called himself a Catholic anarchist. His one peccadillo in this character transformation was the fact that he still religiously read Ezra Pound's poetry, and Pound was an avowed Fascist, one of the enemies, Dermot's friends told him. But he did not care; he loved Pound's poetry, he said, and he would forgive him everything because of those poems.

A half-block away, Dermot attended Monday-night readings and formal readings on Wednesday evenings at the newly opened Poetry Project at St. Mark's Church in the Bouwerie at East 10th Street and Second Avenue. On Tuesdays, he got home from work at the Lincoln Center Music Library where he worked as a clerk, ate his dinner quickly at home (lentils and rice usually), and walked down Second Avenue to East 2nd Street, the Old Courthouse, an abandoned court house that had become part of the Poetry Project as well as a venue for the Bread & Puppet Theatre, the Millennium Archive, and a rehearsal space for Theatre Genesis, where Sam Shepard was beginning to put up his plays. Dermot attended the poetry workshop offered by the Black Mountain poet Joel Oppenheimer, who had become Dermot's literary mentor. Joel was the director of the newly opened Poetry Project, and he had other favorites than Dermot Froidveaux, whom Joel referred to as Cold Veal. Cold Veal could not compare to the director's favorites, who were Scott and Jerry and Tom and Ron and Elaine and Ross and…

But Dermot persisted, whether Joel called him Cold Veal or not.

Writing was nothing if it wasn't hard work.

He had to put in the hard graft, as the Irish called it, and he was Irish.

Well, he was what the Irish called a "plastic paddy," someone who was Irish through a parent or grandparent, not through birth or education or slogging through the culture on a day to day basis. He had a New York accent, to be exact, a Long Island one. He liked to say that he and Walt Whitman spoke the same way, being from Long Island and also the Island's western edge in Brooklyn.

Dermot was Irish via a father he detested and grandparents he had never known. His grandfather had worked in the Brooklyn Navy Yard during the war, and he had died six months before Dermot was born in 1946. His grandmother had died when Dermot's father was only five years old, fresh-off-the-boat, they had come from Ireland by way of Liverpool, and then got off the ship in Nova Scotia, because it was too expensive to go to Boston or New York and, besides, they did not have the proper paperwork to enter the United States.

Instead they had transited from Halifax down through Canada until they got to somewhere south of Montreal and near the Vermont border, which they walked across in the dead of winter in the middle of the night, a five-year-old boy, his sickly mother whose cough had become worrisome, even to her drunken husband, who walked into Vermont in a whiskey and beer haze. His wife would die in Brooklyn several months later.

It was their son, Dermot's father, who would receive a doctored Baptismal certificate, which in turn would become the family's ticket to staying in Brooklyn.

Sometimes Dermot dreamed of his grandmother, who he imagined to be a kind, sweet woman, a seamstress, and rumor had it that she had been a hedge-row teacher in Castlebar, County Mayo, while her husband Bernard Froidveaux was a bounder, as they called them, a man who drifted from place to place and job to job, never amounting to a hill of beans. A man with the scent of whiskey on his breath at all times of day and night. A silent man. Moody. Tempermental. Puglistic in his cups. A man who was not sociable when he drank. A man who got into fights, who misunderstood easily, a man with a lot of demons to haunt him. His grandfather, Dermot thought, would not likely be a man to express an opinion about someone such as Ezra Pound. But so be it.

They (Dermot's grandparents) had met in a pub in Galway.

Bernard, the grandfather, sang a decent song, and the rumor had it that he was a Fenian. He even claimed to be the scion of Francois Froidveaux, a legendary Fenian out of Ennis in County Clare. Francois was not his father, though, but a distant cousin, and the story was that the family were French Huguenots, and that was probably true.

The Froidveaux were tall and thin and had tremendously large noses.

Dermot Froidveaux was tall and thin and had a large nose. People in New York often asked him if he was Jewish.

Dermot's father Aloysius Froidveaux (Bernard's boy) was often asked the same question, because of his extraordinarily large nose. But unlike his ancestors Ally, as he was called, was short and thick in his frame, low to the ground and without any French refinements. Dermot's father worked for the federal government, in the Federal Bureau of Investigation, as an agent. Dermot wanted to have nothing to do with the FBI, the CIA, the feds in general, and any kind of cop or fireman work that the world, before he became a literary man, had in mind for young Dermot Froidveaux.

Reading Ezra Pound's poetry had convinced Dermot that a better, more interesting life awaited him, if only he could persist, despite the setbacks financially and creatively.

At the Poetry Project, Dermot was another face in the crowd. But he listened avidly to what Joel had to say about Robert Creeley and Charles Olson, Denise Levertov and Lorinne Neideker, the Objectivist poets, and of course William Carlos Williams and Ezra Pound. If there were poetic saints, it was the Black Mountaineers, the New York School of Poetry's usual suspects (Frank O'Hara, John Ashbery, Kenneth Koch, Ron Padgett, and Ted Berrigan), and outlying poets such as Louis Zukofsky, George Oppen, and Charles Reznikoff. The two gods were Williams and Pound, and Joel preferred the god from New Jersey, the good doctor, WCW. But he paid a lot of lip service to Ezra Pound, talking about him a great deal and talking around his poetry and his politics and never giving them a good idea of just how far afield Pound had drifted from his brilliant stances in the Teens and the 1920s in Paris amid James Joyce, working with T. S. Eliot, getting Robert Frost published, and finding homes for Ernest Hemingway's stories. There was nobody quite like Pound in those days, generous to a fault and dedicated to getting his friends' work published.

No, Joel wasn't the best mentor or teacher to tell them about Ezra Pound, so Dermot and his friends relied on other sources, including Joel's assistant Sam Abrams who at least had read through all the *Cantos* up to that point.

Pound's influence was everywhere.

You saw it in poems by Gary Snyder, even Frank O'Hara poems.

It was there in poets that the St. Mark's crowd didn't read, such as Robert Lowell and John Berryman, and—it was certainly there in Charles Olson, whose poems seemed as if they were extensions of what Pound had laid down in his voluminous books, especially in *The Cantos*.

Facing Ezra Pound was nothing new to Dermot Froidveaux. He had encountered the poet's *Cantos* five years earlier when he ran away from home at the age of fifteen. He had taken a Nassau County bus into Queens and hopped on the E train at 179th Street in Jamaica, getting off at West 4th Street. During that couple of weeks when he didn't go home to the family's house in New Hyde Park, he found a used but pristine copy of *The Cantos* in a bookshop on East 7th Street, just off of Second Avenue.

It was not a book that was easily revealed, so Dermot discussed his find with a friend name Harry Harlow, one of the smartest boys in his high school. Harlow had already read Pound's poems and loved them. He was a precocious boy, but troubled by his fascination with Neo-Nazis. If you went to his house, a few blocks from Dermot's, Harry's bedroom had a swastika on the wall, and he preached a gospel to Dermot about Pound's obsessions with Mussolini and Jefferson.

Dermot was only interested in the poems, not the politics, which even then he found appalling.

Harry asked to borrow the book for a night, and Dermot acquiesced, lending his friend *The Cantos*, which he would not see again until several months later at which time Harry Harlow gave it back after endless badgering from Dermot.

When Dermot moved to East 10th Street in 1966, he had a party one night and various friends from high school showed up, including Harry Harlow. Somehow Harry got his hands on *The Cantos* again and went off that night back to Long Island with Dermot's copy. It would be another year before Dermot got back his beloved book.

From that point it never left him.

Dermot would buy and sell books, usually doing the latter when he was broke and needed money to eat. He would take his poetry books to the Cornelia Street bookshop. But he got the most money from an old Jewish man on East 4th Street near where Cornelia disgorged into Sixth Avenue. The shop was tiny and could only hold a few people, and the old man always gave Dermot very good prices for his poetry books. But the Pound book was never on offer to the used booksellers in the Village. Somehow Dermot had managed never to part with his Pound book again.

After about a year or two of studying poetry at St. Mark's Poetry Project, Dermot began to write more prose. He drifted away from the poets he knew at the church workshops and began to publish nonfiction in various newspapers downtown, and then he went back to school to finish his degree at City College, where he stayed on to do a masters. Then he went to the Graduate Center, writing his doctorate on Pound's influence on his own generation. Somewhere in his education, he even attended Yale University for a brief time, studying drama. At that time, he met with Ezra Pound's daughter Mary at the Bienecke Library, asking her permission to use the poet's papers housed there. Dermot had convinced himself that he was going to write a play about Pound.

He still remembered those days on the Lower East Side, though, the arguments he and his friends would have in Max's Kansas City and St. Adrian Company bar, their discussions always about alternative poetry, Jack Spicer, John Wieners, Robert Duncan, the names rolled off their tongues in great cascades of speech. It was serious business too. Dermot remembered one night in Max's where the discussion between the New York School of Poets and the Black Mountain poets got out of hand, and a fist fight broke out.

It was silly, that fight, but it showed just how serious they took poetry and poetics and the various poets whom they all read.

Pound and Williams always headed up the hierarchy of poetic need, like Maslow's, only this concerned the pyramid of poetry and who sat at the top of it, and in the 1960s, Williams invariably won out over Ezra Pound.

In the late Sixties, Pound was long out of St. Elizabeths Hospital in Washington, D.C., and had gone back to Italy, first in Rapallo with his wife Dorothy and later in Venice with his mistress Olga Rudge. Venice is where Pound died.

He did not enter
Into silence he said but
Silence entered him

And then words simply failed him—
He knew that it was the end

If there were fights over Ezra Pound, it invariably took place between the Jewish writers and the non-Jewish ones. It usually had nothing to do with the quality of Pound's verse, although people who did not like him claimed that his poetry was not very good either and that his influence was greatly exaggerated. The Jewish writers raised the issue of his anti-Semitic remarks, and they had a point. His radio broadcasts were despicable, to say the least, and deemed treasonous by the American government after the Second World War ended. By the time Dermot was born, Pound was already incarcerated at St. Elizabeths Hospital, although to call it an incarceration is misleading. He was permanently being housed in a mental institution with no likelihood of ever being released into the general population again. You could despise his politics, and yet there was a kind of collective embarrassment that the United States had put away one of its most famous poets. It was something that one might more readily associate with the Soviet Union and their re-education camps for writers, where psychiatry was another name for institutional torture.

Dermot was appalled by Pound's politics, but he loved the poetry and read it obsessively, so no wonder he wrote a doctoral dissertation upon Pound's influence because Dermot saw it everywhere, at the Poetry Project, even at the Jewish Y on Lexington Avenue uptown. He saw it in magazines, in recordings, how people broke their lines or how they used *yr* for *your* and used ampersands (&) instead of writing out the word *and* (and). Pound had invented a thousand little devices in his style that were pretty much the standard fair of alternative poets the country over. More than Williams, Dermot Froidveaux saw Pound as the great influence upon his own generation, but in this opinion, at least downtown in the late 1960s, he was pretty much alone. His friends read and discussed Pound and incorporated some of his interests into their own work, regarding Chinese verse, Confucius, Japanese haiku, Provençal poets, Dante, Guido Cavalcanti, Arnaut Daniel—these were all names that slipped off their tongues as the young poets got drunk in Max's Kansas City or the St. Adrian Company bar down along Broadway near Houston Street (pronounced like the word *house* not like the word *you*, just as downtown New Yorkers did not ever call it Avenue of the Americas but Sixth Avenue). The young poets drank and talked late into the night about William Carlos Williams' *Paterson* and Ezra Pound's *Cantos*. But the people who were really into Pound also talked about his various books, such as *The ABC of*

Reading or *The Spirit of Romance* or his Provençal translations; they talked deep into the night about Kung and the *Analects*, "The Seafarer," various cantos in Dante's *Divine Comedy* or even monetary theories.

—Well, his name is Pound, Dermot said, and he was obsessed with monetary values and currency. His father Homer worked for the mint. Money was a serious subject for Pound.

—Fuck money, one of the poets said.

His name was Jerry and he was Jewish and he was also a junkie, and he happened to know a great deal about Ezra Pound.

—I'm more interested in how Pound created the shorthand of our own poetics, Jerry said, then he ordered a round of drinks for everyone.

The young poets in the bar were wary of Jerry because he was a conman, and a round of drinks from him often entailed a reciprocity that no one was prepared to give him, all of them being broke as sailors who spent their money in port.

—Let me read you a new poem, Jerry said, changing the subject.

He read his poem beautifully; he was a fine poet.

—What does this have to do with Ezra Pound? a poet named Tom said.

Tom was Black and a good Southern poet from Alabama. He was tall and muscular, being an ex-Marine, and he was moments away from his first book being published. Of all the poets at the table in Max's that night, he was probably the one most into Ezra Pound.

—It has diddly-squat to do with Ezra Pound, Jerry said. But we don't have to spend the rest of our lives discussing Ezra Pound.

—Like hell we don't, Tom said.

Jerry grew quiet. Tom was big and tough, and when he challenged you, there was an element of danger in his response.

—Like hell we don't, Tom repeated, also being into the blues, and when you said something once, you needed to say it again, just to create the right measure and beat.

Jerry turned to Dermot and asked him what he liked about Ezra Pound.

—The rhythm of experience, the exact treatment of the object, *le mot juste…*

—Okay, okay, Jerry said. I see where you guys are going with this. Personally I prefer Paul Eluard's poetry to anything Pound ever wrote.

He stood, wearing a dark linen suit, a black shirt and black tie, with a pencil mustache over his upper lip. He looked like a Sicilian hitman more than a poet. He laughed his junkie laugh. Then he put his Panama hat on his head and walked out the door of Max's.

—There's nobody quite like Jerry, Ron said, ordering another round of beers for everyone.

CHAPTER FOUR

"To have gathered from the air a live tradition
or from a fine old eye the unconquered flame
This is not vanity.
Here error is all in the not done,
all in the diffidence that faltered."
—"Canto LXXXI

It was away from the cages, in one of which Ezra Pound languished. Dust in his eyes. Lights in his eyes. A six by six by six foot dungeon. No privacy. He was on exhibit night and day. Finally they had broken him. He was a broken man. He looked old and frail and too vulnerable to be put on trial for treason. There was nothing subtle about how they treated him. His teeth ached; his scalp itched. His clothes were filthy, as if he was an animal, not the man who had introduced Vivaldi to the 20th century. The young soldiers were not educated enough to know who he was or what he had done. They saw him as just another prisoner. But whereas the other prisoners, one by one, were tried summarily and executed, military style, Ezra Pound lingered on and on, the sunlight and the dust grinding him down. No one was quite sure of what his crime was or why he was still in the cage, long after the others had been put to death. If it was treason, it was simple; kill him. And if it was not treason, why, let him go. That's how the soldiers spoke away from their superiors. They said Ez was a nice old guy, a bit odd, a little eccentric, maybe even possibly quite crazy.

The things he said! No one could understand a word of it; you'd need a dictionary by your side just to converse with him about what he wished to eat for breakfast. He was a born teacher, too, always trying to educate the young soldiers about Thomas Jefferson and Dante and other names which no one had ever heard before.

Away from the gorilla cages, there were big tents for the officers, and that was where Harry and Louise were sat talking.

Harry was an intelligence guy. Louise was a nurse. She had just given him a report about the health of the prisoners. They're fine, he said. There are some problems, Louise had said. Harry laughed. They were discussing Ezra Pound. It amazed the stocky, short intelligence guy.

—He thinks that I'm his friend, Harry laughed.

He was a thick man, his neck like a stovepipe, and his hands were meaty. He was big-bellied and broad-chested, though squat, probably no taller than five feet five inches tall, though he did not read like a short man or a small one, but rather a dynamic person, like an old-time boxer. Was he Italian? Yes, he was Italian. But not like any Italian in Italy; Harry was an Italo-American, from Brooklyn, it would turn out. No matter what Harry was, he looked like an Italian, only he had that New York accent, one of the outer boroughs. He had a suit on, a white shirt and tie, dress shoes and socks, and he wore a fedora, even in this dust and heat. His suit was dark and ill-fitting and looked cheap. No Italian would be found dead in such clothing, even in postwar Italy. The Italians had a sense of dressing well, even in their poverty. Not Harry. He had money in his pocket, and yet he dressed like a bureaucratic slob.

Harry was there from the Federal Bureau of Investigation which had dispatched him from their New York office to bring back a prisoner of war named Ezra Pound. Before returning to America with his prisoner, he was supposed to gather as much intelligence as he could regarding the prisoner.

Harry and Louise sat at a field table in front of a field tent.

Of their various prisoners, some were guys who had gone AWOL at key times; others were madmen and murderers. Ezra Pound was an unusual case, or at least Louise was trying to portray him that way to Harry, the FBI agent.

—Have you told him otherwise?

—Otherwise, what?

—That you are not his friend, Louise said.

Like most nurses, Louise was a compassionate person. She had already ministered to Mr. Pound, helping his red and running eyes, giving him medication for his raw throat, finding him a toothbrush and some toothpaste, even cadging some underwear for him to put on. She had managed to get Pound out of the cage to walk around, even to allow him use of a typewriter after the typing pool finished their work for the day.

—The guy can't hear a word I say, Harry said. He's lost in his thoughts. He's nuts. I don't know what the fuck he's saying, but I'm writing it all down in case they need to use it at his trial.

—He's probably on the same page as you are politically.

—I'm not a traitor, Harry said, matter of factly.

—No one said you were, Harry. But Pound's very right wing, and I'm presuming that you, being an FBI guy, are more rightward in your thinking than leftward.

—I don't worry about such distinctions, Harry said, lighting a Camel cigarette and offering Louise one. She declined. He continued: I'm here to do my job. Mr. Pound is not a bad man, I can't fault him for that. But he's full of crazy, foolish ideas, about poetry and finance, economics, history. I just let him go on. I let him dig his own grave.

—Why? Louise asked, with the precision of a philosopher.

—Why?

—Yeah, why?

—I'm an FBI guy.

—So?

Harry smoked his cigarette and stared off into the distant hills around Pisa. He had the familiar look of the combat veterans at the base. That thousand-yard-stare, Louise called it.

—I'm looking for one thing.

—What's that, Harry?

He did not like when she called him Harry. He would have preferred if she called him Mr. Cavalcanti. After all, he was here on business. He wasn't here to flirt with Louise, even if she was a young and attractive nurse and he was still a bachelor sewing his wild oats. The war was serious business, and he had been sent to Italy on serious business, to bring back the poet Ezra Pound for a federal trial on treason for his broadcasts on Italian radio.

Harry looked back at Louise and stuffed out his cigarette.

—A conviction, he said flatly, staring at her.

—For what?

—Treason, he answered.

—That sweet old doddering man?

—He's a Fascist.

Harry sweated in his wool suit in Pisa. His fedora was built for a New York winter, not the sunshine and *dolce far' niente* of Pisa. He had a five-o'clock shadow on his face, and sweat stood out on his brow, where he seemed to have one long dark eyebrow weaving across the top of his face. He smoked one cigarette after another, compulsively, obsessively, with determination. No amount of Louise's humor and softness, attractiveness and flirtatiousness seemed to phase the man, who had this one track mind about getting Ezra Pound convicted for treason. Come on, Harry, Louise said. Lighten up, live and let live. We've had enough war for one lifetime. Forgive and forget.

Being around Ezra Pound turned everyone into a poet, even a prosaic FBI agent such as Harry Cavalcanti.

HARRY. I was sent here
With one purpose:
Collect as much evidence
As possible. Get Ezra Pound
Convicted of treason.

My methods are irrelevant.
It's the results that count.
He's spilling the beans
To me every day I talk to him.
He's digging his own grave.
I know everything about this guy.
His handwriting. His typewriter,
What kind it is—everything!

—That's crazy, Harry. I thought you were a good guy.

HARRY. I am a good guy.
I'm one of the good guys.
He's one of the bad guys.
The good guys get the bad guys
Put away for life or we get them
Convicted of treason,
And hung from the nearest
Poplar tree, where they belong.

LOUISE. Let the old man go.
He's frail, he's distracted.
He's not a bother to anyone.
He's a screwball, that's all.
There isn't a crime for that.
We all need to get home.
I've got a fiancé waiting
For me back in Pittsburgh.

Harry lit another cigarette. He'd already smoked two packs that day. Strong unfiltered Camels. He looked excited. He said:
   —I've got over one hundred specimens of his handwriting.

Instead of being impressed, Louise asked: Have you ever read his poetry?

He was one of those postwar American men who didn't seem to hear women when they spoke to him. Or maybe he only heard what he wanted to hear. In any event, he went on speaking about his specimens, as he called them. He told her that he had over one hundred from Pound's typewriter.

The authorities in Washington had given the word that they did not want Pound broken and frail, an object of sympathy for educated Americans. Get him out of the cage, they said. Put him in a tent. Let him write things on the typewriter. Perhaps he would incriminate himself. They would be pleased that Harry, a middle-range bureaucrat, would have gathered one hundred specimens of the poet's writings.

—Did you know that the "g" on his typewriter sticks?

—No, I didn't know that, Louise said.

She took out a cigarette and lit it, drew in smoke and exhaled a big puff of it.

—I don't like it when dames smoke, he said.

—Really? Louise said. Then why did you offer me a cigarette before?

He did not pick up the sarcasm in her voice. He was not a subtle man. His favorite instrument was the hammer.

—And that matters? Louise asked.

—What?

—Your specimens.

—It could become important, he said.

—Where?

—At his trial.

—You mean to tell me that it's going to become important at his trial about whether or not the fucking "g" sticks on his goddamn typewriter?

Harry said he did not like it when women swore. She grinded out the light at the end of her cigarette with the heel of her shoe. Louise let Harry know in so many words that she did not give a flying fuck what he thought about the way she talked. She had been in this war as a nurse for many years and had witnessed firsthand the death of countless American soldiers, had seen people come in to the operating theatre with limbs missing screaming for morphine, their faces blown off. Who cared if she had a vocabulary like a sailor? So she let Harry know that she did not give a shit what he thought about how women spoke or didn't. She said that she didn't like when men were idiots, especially when they were in positions of power.

It was almost as if Louise had not said a thing.

Harry went on talking about his boxes of evidence for the treason trial he was going to bring Pound back to in America once Harry got the word to bring him back home. He told her that he had fifteen boxes filled with his own notes on Mr. Pound.

—You need a break, Louise said.

Once again he ignored her.

CHAPTER FIVE

"I have curled 'mid the boles of the ash wood,
I have hidden my face where the oak
Spread his leaves over me, and the yoke
Of the old ways of men have I cast aside."
—"La Fraisne"

It was the beginning of the 20th century, the new century. A bunch of them knew each other from their classes at the University of Pennsylvania. There was EP and Bill Williams, and then there was Ez's girlfriend, sixteen-year-old Hilda Doolittle. Bill was a handsome mutt, as Ez called him. A little Puerto Rican. A little English. A Wasp. A Jew. A guy from Rutherford, New Jersey. He told them that he wanted to be a poet but, Bill said, in order to be a poet, he needed to make a living. So I'm planning to be a baby doctor, a general practitioner, Bill Williams said. That's too sensible, Bill, Ezra said. Already Ezra was dressed oddly. That evening he wore a cape and a big slouch hat with a feather. He had on Spanish boots which reached almost to his knees. Both young men had a crush on Hilda, but right then and there Hilda was infatuated with Ezra. His oddness was so appealing, she said to Bill, who had grunted when Ezra was out of the room, searching in his own room for another poem to read to his captive audience.

—Simplest is best, Bill said. Occam's razor.

Just then Ezra came back into the room.

Now he wore a pince-nez.

Hilda adored it.

Bill thought it a bit much, as he did with most things that Ezra did, though Bill would grant that Ezra was a fairly good tennis player.

—To hell with Occam's razor, Ezra shouted.

Sometimes it seemed as though everything Ezra said was said in capital letters. The world is too complex for Occam.

—And beautiful, Hilda said.

She was as beautiful as any woman either man had met. And talented. Already her poems were as good as either one of them were writing.

—And beautiful, Ez said.

—I want to break it down, Bill said. I want to make it as simple as hell.

—Hell is never simple, Wild Bill. Consider Dante.

—Bill is anything but wild, Hilda declared.

By declaring, she was showing the two male poets that she was hanging around with Ezra far too much, because everything for him was a declaration. You would never find Ezra going through even Customs and saying that he had nothing to declare. Everything was declaimed for Ezra, including ordering a meal or asking a friend how they were.

—That's why I call him that.

It's an oxymoron.

Bill needs to break out

Of his mold.

He likes Walt Whitman.

BILL. I love Walt Whitman.

EP. Then unhinge the door

From its hinges.
Kick out the jams!

BILL. I'm busy with my studies
In pre-med. I have an anatomy
Test this afternoon.
        The jams
Will have to wait.
        At least, I can't kick them

Out
Until later in the week
Or maybe not until

Next week.

EP. Seize the day, Williams.
If you had more Europe
In you,
You'd understand
That injunctive.

BILL. There's plenty of Europe
In me, Ezra.

EP. You're an Amurkan mutt, Williams.
Aren't you even a little
I don't know what to call it
Not quite a Jew, just a little—
Jewish?

BILL. Be careful, Ezra.

EP. About what?

BILL. I don't like it when you talk about race
And ethnicity, about the Jews and the
Gentiles and all that rubbish.
There is no such thing as race.

EP. Says who?

Ezra had a way of inciting Bill, and Bill often took the bait. Bill was as brilliant as anyone, and yet Ezra had a way of trying to put him in his place and to suggest that he was less American than Ezra was. Hilda just wanted to go out and have some fun. Men could sometimes be such thick-headed beasts, even the poets. Everything was a competition with the men, and Hilda detested competition. She detested war and competition. After poetry, what was there? The arts and culture; this is what America needed. It needed inspiration from Europe, and then maybe it could find its own rhythms, its own voice. Even Ezra could be as thick as two planks.

—Let's get ready for the masquerade dance, Hilda Doolittle said. It's Halloween, you two, why are you arguing?

Bill Williams had on his serious face, his future doctor's face.

—Race is a man-made invention, he said. We're all descended from Africa.

—Not the Pounds, Ezra said.

He said it more to antagonize Bill and less because he believed it.

—Where are the Pounds descended from? she asked her beau.

—From Philadelphia, my darling, and before that, it was New England, and before that, England, and before that...

—Africa, Bill Williams said. We are all descended from a common ancestor in Africa.

Hilda decided to ignore her two male friends.

—I'm going to the dance as a Venetian courtesan. No, I think I'll go as Sappho.

—Sappho? Bill asked.

—I'm translating her, Hilda declared.

—That's a great idea, Hilda, Bill said, but then Ezra stole the spotlight once again.

—I'm going to go as my future self, Ezra said.

—Who is that? Bill inquired of his friend.

—A famous poet.

Ezra wore his cape, his big hat with a feather in the band, his Spanish boots upon his feet. He was something else, Ezra Pound. Bill tried to say that a poet didn't have to look like that. Ezra just laughed malignantly at the idea that he could be a poet and someone simultaneously conventional and normal seeming.

Bill loved poetry, but he saw nothing wrong with being conventional to a certain extent. He planned to become a doctor, a GP, with a specialization in pediatrics. At least that is why he was enrolled at the University of Pennsylvania, to affect that professional transformation.

Why does a poet have to look a certain way? Bill Williams was there to challenge his flamboyant friend.

—Why does a poet have to look a certain way? Bill asked.
—This is heresy, Wild Bill.
—Then so be it.

EP. (To HD) Bill is writing in something
He has called
The American Idiom.

BILL. Out of the mouths of Polish mothers
In Rutherford, New Jersey,
Where one day I will set up
My medical practice,
Attending to the delivery of
Their babies.

EP. My inspiration is the troubadours.
Arnaut Daniel. Pere Vidal.
I am not settled on Walt Whitman.
I prefer Dante. Guido Cavalcanti.

HD. I'm going as Sappho.
It's decided.

EP. And how will Sappho go?

HD. Something sheer, transparent,
Gossamer. Diaphonous.

EP. How will I contain myself?

HD. You are a Philadelphia gentleman.

EP. We are all gentleman

At the University of Pennsylvania.
That's the problem.
We need a few more troubadours
Among us.

(Pause)

Both Hilda Doolittle and Ezra Pound wanted to know what William Carlos Williams was going to go as? What costume had he settled upon? Bill said that he thought he might go as a pre-med student worried about his anatomy exam.

—That way I could go as myself, he said.

—You could go as a Puerto Rican, Ezra said. Aren't you a little bit that?

Bill was not amused.

—Careful, he warned his friend Ezra Pound. I know you're kidding me, but I don't like it when you go there.

Ezra could not leave it alone.

—Or you could go as a Jewish rug merchant from the Middle East.

Hilda sensed that Bill was not best pleased.

—Leave Bill alone and let's get ready, she said.

Ezra walked to the door and said that he would be right back.

—I'm sorry with how Ezra treats you

Sometimes. It embarrasses me.
I know he loves you as a friend
And fellow poet. He tells me how much

He likes your poetry and your spirit.
He predicts great things for you
One day in the not too distant future.

BILL. Sometimes he crosses the line.
I don't know what to do about it.
Who cares about his dumb purity
Of ethnicity or whatever he gets on about.
So I'm Puerto Rican. So I'm Jewish.
I'm a lot of things. I'm probably
As English as Ezra is, maybe even
More because of my father
Coming from there.

**(EP enters theatrically, wearing
his cape, his big hat with a plume,
his Spanish boots)**

EP. I'm going as Pere Vidal!

Chapter Six

"Invitation, mere invitation to perceptivity
Gradually led him to the isolation
Which these presents place
Under a more tolerant, perhaps, examination."
   —"The Age Demanded"

They were in Paris, walking around in the autumn air, leaves of many colors on the ground, a damp chill and gray skies anticipating the winter just around the corner. They were both of them bundled up in overcoat (Joyce) and cape (Pound), hats on their heads, big wool scarves wrapped around their necks, hangman's style. Pound's massive wool scarf consisted of several Chinese characters, a language that Joyce, master of many tongues, had not yet dabbled in. He would need, he said, to exhaust his fascination with Greek and Latin, Romance languages and German, Slavic tongues and Irish, before he could tackle Chinese characters the way his friend Ezra Pound had. They walked, the two writers, briskly through the damp air, purposeful in their gaits, and searching, Joyce said, for a place to get a drink. Hair of the dog, Jimmy called it. He wore kid gloves and dark glasses to protect his delicate eyesight from the ravages of the light. Joyce to Pound:

—That takes the solitary, unique, and, if I may so call it, *recherché*, biscuit.

And Pound back at Joyce, because Ezra understood the reference immediately, after all, he was an aficionado of *Dubliners*, so his answer was this:

—"Two Gallants."

—"Two" it is, Ezra.

—And two gallants are we, Pound said.

Joyce went along with the game.

—And if I am Lenehan, Joyce said, then you must be Corley.

—Where's me slavey? Pound asked, laughing wickedly.

—Just around the bend, Pound, Joyce answered, being a person who knew how to control a mob of one.

—Only just, said Ezra, laughing still.

Now they both laughed.

Then they were silent.

Joyce often was that, silent, that is, though Pound was rarely silent, that being a condition he abhorred in himself. Pound was nothing if not a garrulous American, albeit a brilliant one, Joyce thought, and a savvy one. Mr. Joyce often thought that if one could point a finger toward the one person who influenced all aspects of Modernism, it was Ezra Pound, his companion of the moment in Paris. But silence was one thing that separated the two literary figures, as Pound did not care for it, and Joyce embraced it as if it were a beautiful Dalmatian woman wearing a mink shawl and feathery hat on a boulevard in Trieste.

The author, at that time, of *Dubliners* and *Ulysses*, had a way of expanding silence and turning it into a form of music and even letting it become a philosophical statement. Silence was a device for Joyce; it was part of his bag o' tricks, including alliteration, assonance, similes, metaphors, and, like Dante himself hisself, allegory. For wasn't what Joyce did, a long, elaborate contemporary allegory?

It was as though Ezra Pound had read Joyce's authorial mind. He said.

—It is more than allegory.

—What is more than allegory? Joyce asked.

—The *fecking* books you write, Joycey.

—Me *fecking* books? asked Joyce.

—If it was no more than allegory, James Stephens could finish up the work-in-progress for you, Pound declared.

Pound often declared, and when he was declaring, he declaimed. He rarely just spoke about anything, even when he ordered a sandwich on a street in Paris.

Joyce looked slightly alarmed.

—I have told James Stephens that he is to complete any book I have left unfinished upon my termination as a sentient being, Poundie.

—That would be the exception to the Poundian rule regarding the allegorical in said Joycean oeuvre.

—Orb?

—Oeuvre! Pound shouted.

—In that case, Pound, Joyce said, make my eggs a bit less runny this time.

Joyce fell silent again.

This time he looked exhausted.

Then after a time, as if getting a second wind, he spoke again.

—There is one thing about Paris which sucks.

—What is that, Joycey?

—Their *fecking* eggs and toast.

—Ah, said Pound.

—Ugh, said Joyce. It is an abomination. Why can't anyone make a decent fry-up? Two eggs, a bit less runny, and toast, thank you, that is not burnt to look like Cardinal Ugolino's arse.

—Ugolino's arse?

Pound near spit up on himself.

—Yes, Joyce said, burnt toast that resembles Ugolino's arse. And I am not being allegorical, Ezbo. I am stating a fact. An obvious fact. The toast in Paris sucks.

—But otherwise you are copacetic with the capitol of the world?

—My children miss Trieste.

—Your children?

—Yes, Giorgio and Lucia.

—What is it they miss?

—They are Triestians, born and bred. Well, at least bred.

Pound thought for a moment.

—What does a Triestino miss when in Paris, Joyce?

—Presnitz, Joyce said.

—Presnitz?

—Yes, presnitz. Also, they like to speak the imperfect Italian of their native city.

—And their mother? Pound asked.

He knew that the way to Joyce's heart was to ask after Nora, even though Pound, personally, found her a bit dull or maybe not so much dull as analphabet. Her stories were good enough when she spoke, Pound thought, but she lacked book-reading knowledge and/or curiosity. She lacked a vocabulary in French and the Florentinian rhythms of Italian. Like her children, she spoke Triestino Italian, a kind of merchant-class Italian that seemed more Austro-Hungarian than Mediterranean.

But it was always wise to ask after Nora and their children if you wished to remain on Joyce's good side and not wind up on his bad side, i.e., Joyce's shit list.

—And Nora? Pound repeated his question. How does she be?

—She be a queen bee in her hive, Joyce said. She be co-pacetic with the daily grind of Paree and the quotidian elements of her being, day to fecking day.

—And yourself? Pound asked. How y'all be?

—I all be good, Joyce stated. But me arse hurts from hemispheric hemorrhoids, me toids drop like gas bombs. Me eyes are becoming like the bats. Which makes me feel bat-shit crazy, Pound. I probably need yet another fecking operation...

—Oy, Jaesus! Pound shouted.

—Yes, take that name in vain, Ezra. And besides me bloody fecking eyes, I have no more room for me books, no room for me suits and shoes, no room for family visiting from Doubloon. No room for new underwear or a new chair.

—No room at the inn, said Pound.

—No fecking room, said Joyce.

Then he fell silent.

They sat in one of Joyce's favorite cafes, and he loved to sit in this particular café when it rained in Paris, and it was raining all over Paris that day. The café was called Hamlet's Ghost, and it was run by a London Irishman who had read all of the master's works to date, including parts of the work-in-progress that Pound had managed to get published in various Parisian literary magazines.

There were many different ghosts in the café, Father Hamlet only being one of them, though Hamlet the Son was nowhere to be seen. His ghost remained in Elsinore where there was the constant smell of old, tired fish in Denmark.

Paris smelled of rain and earth and flowers in the springtime, which happened to be the season in which this encounter took place. Otherwise Joyce would have been wearing an expensive tweed overcoat that someone or other—the Irish connections—had brought over from Dublin, from Kevin and Howling on Nassau Street, a tweed to take the damn chill out of the air, Joyce said, sitting in the springish café in a gray suit, wearing a white shirt and a tie, his Italian fedora, and his wire-rimmed glasses over his terribly myopic eyes. On his feet he wore a pair of patent leather pumps that he had brought with them from Trieste and later Zurich. They were nearly worn out by now, but they had great sentimental value for Joyce, which explained why he still wore them.

Pound had been trying to get Joyce to buy a sensible pair of shoes that would allow him to walk less painfully through the streets of Paris, but to no avail. The Irish author still wore the patent leather pumps, which he had called "the Pope loafers."

It was actually the first day of spring, and only a few days earlier Joyce had indulged himself in a bit too much Irish whiskey to drink on St. Paddy's Day, which Joyce both liked and disliked, for a variety of reasons. He often said that he did not appreciate sentimentality in literature but he found it perfectly acceptable in real life. Thus St. Paddy's Day had been indulged to the hilt, and now, several days later, Joyce was still feeling a bit rough around the edges. As regard St. Paddy's, he bitched and moaned about it, comparing it to a parade of cops down Fifth Avenue in New York City, he told Pound, but since it was the first day of spring, he tried to be more pleasant.

He looked at his pumps and declared that only a very corrupt Pope would wear such a pair of patent leather shoes.

Pound was not fast enough with the uptake in the conversation, so Joyce once again fell into his proverbial silence. It descended upon the table like a dark rain cloud. All that could be heard from the café was the sound of taxi cabs and lorries, honking horns and grinding gears, the spring-laden trees full of new leaves and city birds: robins, sparrows, starlings, finches, even the hungry raptor perched on a high ledge across from the café.

—How are you? Pound asked, which was another way of asking how much money did Joyce need to stay alive and well in Paris.

—The piper must be paid, Joyce said. The piper and the shoemaker, the butcher and the grocer, not to mention the tailor and the candlestick maker.

Pound removed an envelope filled with French currency, the coin of the realm, but as folding money. He pushed the envelope towards Joyce who pushed it back to Ezra,

Joyce saying that he could not take such largesse from his good friends who, after all, had done so much for Joyce and Co., including removing them from their poverty and ination of Middleurop.

Paris was their oyster, and the oyster demanded certain rituals, this push and pull of the envelope filled with money being one of those rites of passage. Joyce pushed the money bag back to Pound; Pound sent it back in Joyce's direction. They had done this ritual many times, probably twenty or thirty times, the Joyces being perpetually broke or, put another way, they were broke, then got some money from Pound, and would go out spending it extravagantly on clothes and dining out.

Back and forth the envelope went.

Joyce said he could not take it; Pound insisted that he do.

Eventually Joyce capitulated, stuffing the envelope into the inner chest pocket of his suit jacket, and then ordered serious drinks for both of them, whereupon Joyce's mood elevated and he saluted the health of Ezra Pound, the peculiar American who had become the Joyce family's lifeline in Paris.

There were many benefactors to thank. Pound was merely the conduit through which the largesse flowed. Ezra had a gift for relieving wealthy men and women of their funds to support projects such as James Joyce.

—You are most generous, Ezra, Joyce said.

—It ain't me, Joyce, Pound said. It's the rich blue-haired ladies, the Cambridge art ladies. That's who loves you and gives me shedsful of money to pass your way.

—Then god love the blue-haired ladies.

—To the blueheads! Pound shouted, wishing James Joyce were not so profoundly blind because Ezra hungered to play a game of tennis, but instead remained anchored to the café table, tethered to the wonderful words that James Joyce released into the world.

—It is so good to see you, Ezra, Joyce said, fingering the money purse inside his suit jacket.

—And you, Pound said. And you, Jimmyjoyce.

—Ah, said Joyce. The springtime of the spirit has finally come among us. The harbingers are everywhere.

—Where? Pound asked.

Joyce pointed towards the prostitutes gathering across the road at a nearby café.

—Yes, Pound said. Spring's harbingers are everywhere.

—Ah, Joyce said, taking out a pack of cigarettes, offering one to Pound, who refused, so that Joyce placed the proffered cigarette in his own mouth, lit it by striking a wooden match's head on the fly zipper of his trousers. He inhaled the smoke, exhaled a cloud of it from his lungs, coughed dramatically, but only slightly, then grew silent once again.

—Ah, Pound said, trying to sound like Joyce.

Pound was a great imitator, though he would call it part of the allusion. He was paying homage to Mr. Joyce.

—Ah, said Joyce, more authentically, then thanking his friend for keeping the Joyce family alive and well in Paris.

—Apparitions of these faces in the crowd, Joyce said.

—Petals on a wet black bow, returned Pound, though he had long ago given up any affection he might have harbored for that little poem where even the title, "In a Station of the Metro," worked a vivid overtime to accomplish the complete effect of the poem.

—Ah, said Joyce.

Pound answered him by saying:

—That takes the solitary, unique, and, if I may so call it, *recherché* biscuit.

—Indeed, said Joyce.

A waiter came over to fill their glasses again.

The birds sang in the plain trees. Paris was alive with people and traffic. Spring had arrived moments earlier.

CHAPTER SEVEN

"The slough of unamiable liars,
bog of stupidities,
malevolent stupidities, and stupidities,
the soil living pus, full of vermin,
dead maggots begetting live maggots,
slum owners,
usurers squeezing crab-lice, pandars to authority…"
        —"Canto XIV"

H e's got an Everest, Harry said.
        —Who? Louise said and: What?

—Everest. Model 90, serial no. 27780.

—What the hell are you talking about, Harry?

—His typewriter.

—His typewriter?

—The "e" is misaligned.

—So?

Harry beamed. He lit another cigarette off of the flame of the previous butt. They sat on a bench in front of the ubiquitous field tents that were reserved for dignitaries and officers. Harry was neither, but he did work for the FBI. Louise was a nurse, and a pretty one, so the soldiers tended to cut her more slack than they did for the others in the camp. If she wanted to sit on a bench in front of an officer's camp, no one was going to stop her.

—I interviewed the salesman in Rapallo who sold Pound his Everest typewriter.

—And what does that prove? Louise asked in a flustered voice.

—He bought it in 1938, Harry said flatly.

—Give me a fuckin' break! Louise shouted.

Once again Harry noted that he did not approve of women speaking that way.

—Listen, man, I'm a fucking nurse.

I've attended men with half their bodies blown off.

I've had to nurse guys screaming in pain or hallucinating

That they were still in combat.

I don't give a shit what anyone thinks

About the way I use language. In that sense, I guess

I'm like our prisoner, Mr. Pound.

(Pause)

Do you know what your British friends

In intelligence would call what you are doing?

They would say that you are overegging

The pudding. That's what it is:

You're overegging the fuckin' pudding.

He ignored Louise's passionate objections.

—I have samples in black and blue ink. We confiscated the typewriter, an Olympia, that he used to write his radio speeches on, the speeches that he broadcast to the world, giving comfort to the enemy. We have that typewriter from the Ministry of Popular Culture in Rome. We have specimens of scripts, notes, files, articles, even letters. We even have a letter from Mussolini himself to Mr. Pound.

—Mussolini was a douche bag.

—I don't think that is the right way to speak about someone such as Mussolini. A lady doesn't talk that way.

Louise smiled in a smoldering, vicious way at Harry. She smiled like a Hollywood ingénue.

—What makes you think I'm a lady?

Harry gave her remark some thought.

—Other than your way of talking, you seem like a proper dame.

She explained that three years of working in the war in Europe had exposed her to everything that was humanly possible. She said that not only was she not a lady, she wasn't even sure if she was even a human being anymore. Harry was back to her bureaucratic babble. He mentioned dates and initials on "specimens" that he had collected. He had Mr. Pound initial and counter-date them.

LOUISE. He's old,
He's a poet.
Let him go home.
Leave him alone.
If he doesn't want
To return to America,
Let him go back to Rapallo.
His wife wants to see him.
He told me one day.
She's waiting for him
Back in Rapallo.
She's a proper English woman.

HARRY. We're letting her see him today.

LOUISE. So what's the problem?

HARRY. I think he's writing code
When he gives her drafts
Of his poetry.

LOUISE. Code?

HARRY. Those *Cantos* are what
He calls them. They don't make
Any real sense, which is why
I know that they are code.
Listen!

(Picks up some papers, and reads aloud)

— "The enormous tragedy of the dream in the peasant's shoulders." Now what is that supposed to mean?

LOUISE. I don't know.
It's poetry.
I don't think it's supposed to
Make sense or mean
Anything, Harry.

HARRY. Everything has to mean something.

LOUISE. Says who?

HARRY. God.

LOUISE. God said that everything

Is supposed to mean
Something?

HARRY. More or less.

LOUISE. Where did God say this?

HARRY. The Bible.

LOUISE. Where?

(Pause)

Harry was back to business. He noted that he had gotten Pound to admit that he was the author of those various books. Louise laughed, deep from her belly. Her laugh seemed to mock Harry and his need to codify everything.

LOUISE. Of course he's the author
Of the various books. His name
Is on the cover of each and every one
Of them, Harry.

HARRY. He's our asset.
We have to preserve him
From harm or suicide,
And that's why he is
No longer in the cage.
It was inhumane.
It broke his spirit.
We were bringing back
A broken man to face trial.
Now I am mending him.

I'm like his shrink.
He talks to me; he feels better.
He is getting well,
And once he is well enough,
We fly him back to the US
For his trial for treason.

LOUISE. I still say
That he's nothing more
Than a nice old man,
A bit eccentric,
But from what I hear
He's a decent poet.
He knows about forty languages.

HARRY. Nine.

LOUISE. What are they?

HARRY. Chinese. French. Italian.
English (of course), Spanish.
Latin. Greek. German, oh yes,
And Provençal, whatever that is.

LOUISE. They spoke it
In the south of France.

HARRY. Well, they don't speak it now.

LOUISE. No one speaks Aramaic anymore either.
But that is the language of your God.

HARRY. Who?

LOUISE. Who? Jesus Christ.
Listen, Harry, Mr. Pound
Reads your nonsense that you write
Down about him and he signs
What you call your "specimens."
Why can't you leave it at that?

Harry seemed to be boiling alive inside of his wool suit and his fedora, his five-o'clock shadow and his sweaty palms. He told Louise that he could not leave it alone. It was his job to gather such evidence. He had orders. From Washington.

—Who specifically?

—Not at liberty to share that with you. It's all the way up the chain of command.

He banged on about evidence. The need for two witnesses for every act of treason for which Pound was going to be charged. The courts needed meticulous details, he said, to join up the dots and to make the indictment stick.

—They tell me that I can't be vague and general. I need to be specific. But how can I find two people who watched Pound produce a manuscript?

—You're fucked.

Once again Harry repeated that he did not like talk like that. He said that he wished she would refrain from speaking like that to him.

—Like I said, man, I'm not a woman.

—What are you?

—I have no idea.

(Pause)

HARRY. Mrs. Pound is due
To see her husband.

LOUISE. I need to check some of my patients.

(They exit)

Chapter Eight

"I have seen fishermen picnicking in the sun,
I have seen them with untidy families,
I have seen their smiles full of teeth
and heard ungainly laughter."
    —"Salutation"

Ezra's parents' apartment was in the downtown of Rapallo, where Pound himself used to live, though lately he preferred the hill community just above the town. His parents had even learned to speak Italian, a little, and were enthusiastic about this little gem of a town on the Italian Riviera. They were right on the water, a lovely view. The *passeggiata*. Every day around four o'clock the Pounds, Homer and Isabel, as American as Bible study and chocolate chip cookies, joined in the long stroll everyone took along the promenade and down the main streets with the shops just opened after the long afternoon naps everyone seemed to take. The women put on their make-up and their best dresses; the men, in the autumn and winter, wore red trousers and pale tan suede jackets and wore sporty English caps made of tweed. The Pounds loved this four-o'clock ritual and partook of it daily, not able to imagine themselves living anywhere else, although Ezra had been trying for years to get them to come to Italy to live. He told his parents that it was cheaper, and their standard of living would elevate greatly now that they were living on a fixed income after Homer retired. Ezra had tried, over the years, to get his parents to come to Italy when his father retired, but he hadn't counted on there being a World War that would pin them down in the town. They had come to Rapallo in the 1930s, throwing in the towel in their community just outside of Philadelphia. Over the years, Ezra had also tried to get various friends to come to Rapallo, not just to visit, but to live. There was a time when Hemingway was there; and Eliot visited often enough that Ezra thought he might retire there too. But at the end of the day neither friend accommodated Ezra's wish for them to be nearby. He had that only-child syndrome in which he needed his parents and his friends nearby. *Qui vicino*, he called it.

—Homer, he said to his father, *qui vicino* is the only way family should live.

Homer laughed.

Sometimes his son seemed like the genius his father always thought he was, and sometimes he didn't recognize who his son was or had become. Like Homer and his wife Isabel , they disparaged various peoples, the Jews, especially, whom they liked to blame for every ill in the world. That part of Ezra's personality they understood. But Homer, who worked for the U.S. Mint, never quite understood what his son was getting on about regarding the boy's theories on money.

And Homer was not a big fan of Mussolini's.

Now even a place of such beauty and abundance as Rapallo had been for them suddenly had become war-weary, the shops full of empty shelves and shortages. Bread one day. Wine the next. Vegetables another day. Meat almost always.

It was hard to know what was happening anywhere.

The U.S. was at war with Japan and Hitler's Germany, but were they also at war with Italy? If the Pounds listened to their son's broadcasts, they were even more confused. Ezra did not always make sense. But then again he was a poet and he had lectured his parents since he was a boy about what poetry was. He liked to tell them that it was news that stayed news. Then he might say that a poem didn't have to make sense; it only had to be. Of course, there were other concerns than meaning with regard to a poem. Ezra had told them that it involved imagery, the direct treatment of the object, the rhythm of experience, and from Flaubert, their son had gleaned that notion of *le mot juste*. But poetry did not put bread on the table for any of them, not Ezra, not his parents, not Ezra's wife, nor his mistress Olga, both of the women living at Olga's place in the foothills.

Ezra had come down from the hills to see his parents. He told them that he would be going to Rome to do another broadcast, and while he was there, he would look into finding meat, vegetables, olive oil, garlic, parsley, better pasta, wine—all the necessities of life.

They were eternally grateful to their son.

He was a fine boy. He knew how to take care of his family. He knew how to get business done. Wasn't he the center of attention in Paris twenty years ago? He spoke and understood many languages, living and dead. He was good at Latin and Greek, and he knew most of the Romance languages quite well. He was a real scholar of Provençal, the troubadours, that Medieval form of poetry which so influenced

Dante Alighieri, whom their son had taught them, many years ago, was the greatest poet of all time.

—Cavalcanti and Vidal and Arnaut Daniel and so many other troubadours were right behind Dante, in fact, Ezra said, these were all Dante's influences.

But you couldn't eat poetry or wear it like a garment, which you could do with a field of flax. You could weave a shirt or a jacket or a pair of trousers from it or you could turn it into an edible part of the meal. Poetry did not have the versatility of flax, did it? Homer had asked his son rhetorically.

—Men die each day, Pound said to his father Homer, for a lack of what is found in the poem. Bill Williams says that, Dad.

—Bill was such a fine boy. How is he doing?

—Still the doctorly provincial.

—Is he still working in New Jersey?

—Forever, padre.

—His poems are so concise, Homer said, and easy to read.

—Ease of reading is not a criteria to apply to great poetry. My own *Cantos* are not easy to read, and yet they may outlast everyone.

—When you explain them to me, I understand, Homer said. But when I try to read them on my own, I can't make sense of it. Your friend Jimmy Joyce, I have the same problem with *Ulysses*, Ez. *Dubliners* I found beautiful, a steely, righteous prose.

—*Ulysses* is already the greatest literary achievement in

prose of this century or maybe any century, Papa.

—What do I know, right. I'm an old man. I worked in the mint. I understand money. Poetry is another matter or this new kind of prose that Joyce writes. I prefer your friend Hemingway's works. Now there I understand what he is saying. I get it. It is clear and simple and beautiful.

—Well, at least you are not battering me with Amy Lowell. That would be insufferable, *mon pere.*

Pound's mother Isabel walked into the room

—What a surprise!

—I was worried about you, her son said. I'm sorry not to come visit you more often.

—Well, thank you, his mother said.

—For what?

—For thinking of us, his father said.

—I think about you all the time, their son confessed.

—That's sweet, son, his mother declared and came over and hugged him and gave him a big kiss, not as if he were a man in his late fifties, which he was, but a young boy still in their charge.

—You're all I have, Ezra said.

His father begged to differ. He said: Well, there is Dorothy and Omar.

How is Omar?

—He's safe.

Omar was living in the U.K. He was Dorothy's son, and was the reason why Ezra had come down from the hills, leaving his wife Dorothy and his mistress Olga in the hills. He wanted to speak to his parents about Omar.

—Hitler's been bombing London, his mother Isabel said.

She and Homer were the perfect image of the American family. They were retired, and yet they were still engaged and vital.

—Hitler's all right. Ezra said.

—How is Hitler all right?

—Sound monetary system, Ezra declared, that mad gleam in his eye.

His father understood. He had worked in the mint all his life. His name was Pound. He knew a thing or two about who was not the full shilling and who was all right. Homer agreed that a sound monetary system was important. His son Ezra had already explained to the father about Mussolini's sound monetary ways. Now the Axis powers were all on the same page. There were sound fiduciary values. It was important to have your finances in good order. That was how Homer was able to retire, leave America, and settle in Italy just before the war. Of course, he hadn't counted on a World War breaking out. He hadn't figured in what such a war would do to the economy, and how difficult it would make it to get his retirement money and accessing his various financial accounts back in the United States. Homer liked to say to Ezra that money was a very serious business, right up there with poetry and literature.

—Our name is our destiny, Homer laughed.

—It's a good thing our name wasn't Pugh.

Homer laughed again.

It was good to see Ezra, no matter what the circumstances were. Isabel still loved Ezra and treated him like she did when he was a boy. In many respects, even though he was nearly sixty years old, he would always be a kind of precocious child for her.

—Is this where I got my obsession for economics? he asked his mother, who smiled that loving smile of an adoring mother.

—You got your genius for poetry from us.

—And music, Homer said.

EP. And music.
And poetry.
And love of family.
And love of Italy.
And love of life.

HOMER. And the wife.

EP. Yes, love of that too.

(Pause)

His mother Isabel said: We've always gotten along so well as a family.

Pound agreed.

—That's why I brought you to Italy. But I didn't know that war would break out, else I would have left you in Philadelphia, where it is safer and better for your health.

His mother was far more practical than either Homer or Ezra.

—Shall I make us some tea? she asked. I found some

nice breads this morning, and I have some jam that a friend sent.

Their son, Dorothy's and Homer's son, Ezra by name, was impatient, though.

—This is only a short visit, said Ezra.

—Where have you been? Homer asked his son.

—I go to Rome a lot, said Ezra.

—For what? his father asked.

—I record broadcasts for Rome radio.

His mother said: We actually hear your broadcasts, son.

Then his father explained that they didn't know where he went to make the broadcasts that they did hear. But they did listen to the broadcasts when they could, his mother said.

—We hear you loud and clear, his father said.

—But we do hear you, his mother Isabel said.

And then Homer repeated his words again.

—Loud and clear, he said.

Isabel got up and smiled at her son.

—I'll make some the tea, she said. It will only be a minute.

She walked off, the perfect housewife, Homer thought. The perfect mom, thought Ezra. He loved his mother. He loved his father. They did nothing but encourage him his whole life. In many respects, he could do nothing wrong. He was the perfect son. Well, they acted like he was the perfect son, never criticizing his choices, strange as they seemed at times; and they always encouraged his writings, even when neither had a clue what he was saying.

—Poetry's beyond my remit, his mother once said.

—Poetry is what I aspire to, his father claimed. I need more poetry in my life.

The Pounds laughed.

They were a good-natured lot, very American, very down-to-earth. Real. Not pious. Not an ounce of that religious stuff. They were hard-working and simple, smart and people of few words.

While Isabel was in the kitchen, Homer asked his son what brought him to visit his parents at this juncture. Ezra confessed that he hadn't seen either of them in quite some time. But Homer knew his son well, so he said that he knew that something was on Ezra's mind. What was it? Ezra finally admitted that there was something on his mind. Homer reminded him that the family kept nothing from one another. They shared the good and the bad and the ugly and the great.

—Nothing, Ezra said, not as though he were declaring an absence of something to talk about, but rather echoing his father's word earlier, in which it was said that the family kept nothing from each other. Homer again stated something he said to his son repeatedly over the years. They all had a good relationship with one another. Ezra concurred; he told his father that their relationship was great.

—Is it politics? Homer asked.

—Is what politics, Dad?

Then:

—No, it ain't politics, Ezra said in his ersatz down-home accent.

Then his father asked if Dorothy was all right. Did she like living in the hills above Rapallo in Sant'Ambrogio? Dorothy was fine, Ezra told his Dad.

—She feels a bit isolated because of the war. But we all feel isolated.

Homer smiled at his son. He liked Ezra's wife Dorothy a great deal and wished that he and Isabel saw more of her, especially since they were all living in or just outside of Rapallo.

—Tell her to visit us, son. Your mother adores her.

Dorothy loved Mom too, Ezra told his father.

—She loves you and Mom. She's a devoted daughter-in-law.

These words pleased Homer no end. Sometimes he worried that Ezra did not care enough about his wife. He told his son that Dorothy was fine British stock, but Ezra already knew that. That was why he married her. She was fine British stock.

—The finest, Ezra said. She's a Shakespear.

Homer noted that not too many people could make that claim.

The father and son fell into a familiar silence, without any awkwardness. It was the silence that a family had that was satisfied with itself. They sat in chairs facing each other in the parlour.

—So? Homer said.

—So there is something—

Ezra was uncertain about where to begin, which was odd, because amid his parents, these were the two people whom he felt most relaxed with, most himself.

—You wish to talk to me about—

—Yes, Dad.

Homer gestured towards the kitchen with his head nodding in that direction.

—Would you like your mother present?

Ezra laughed.

—That's all right.

He thought and thought, then said:

—Sounds like a plan, Homer admitted.

There was a silence broken only by Homer clearing his throat, then saying that Isabel and he really loved living in Rapallo. It was the best move they had ever made. Ezra smiled, for after all, it was his constant urging that brought his parents to this Riviera of Italy. Homer told Ezra that Rapallo was a fine place to retire. Rent was cheap; food was good; expenses were kept to a minimum. If they got ill, there were some good doctors nearby. He even admitted that while he had struggled initially with learning Italian, now he was beginning to enjoy using this new language. It was so colorful and it had a beautiful cadence and sound.

Ezra pointed out, too, that the war had not really come to Rapallo.

—At least not yet, Ezra added.

—Is that what you're worried about? Homer asked. That the war is going to come to Rapallo and affect your mother and me.

—I worry about it, Homer's son confessed.

—Well, Homer said, we're all right. We're fine.

—Good, good, Ezra said, then he fell untypically silent. He brooded about how to say this.

Finally:

—Dad?

—Son.

—There is something—

—What?

—Things have happened, Ezra said, as foggily and as obscurely as he could be.

Homer shrugged.

—Like what? Like you have a nigger mistress or something.

—No, no, Ezra laughed. Nothing like that. This is between Dorothy and me.

Homer sat up.

—Is Dorothy all right? Is that why we haven't seen her lately? Tell me, boy.

There was no simple way to put it, so he might as well just say it aloud, plain and simply. But the words were not there, they were not on the tip of his tongue.

—Homer is not my son, Ezra said.

—Homer? Homer asked.

—I mean, I mean, damnit to hell, Omar. I mean Omar, Dad.

Homer's expression looked startled.

—Omar?

Now that the cat was out of the bag, Ezra opened the floodgates.

—Dorothy had an affair in Egypt, Ezra told him matter-of-factly.

—An affair?

Ezra explained that it was all right with him; he did not mind if Dorothy had an affair. He certainly had his share of them too.

This was not a region of discourse in which Homer was comfortable. He tried his best to be open and to encourage his son in everything he did. But the idea of having an affair was not in Homer's spirit and sense of how to live a life. Then it dawned on Homer:

—So we are not Omar's real grandparents.

—Correct, Ezra answered.

—That's a shock, Homer confessed.

Ezra waited a beat.

—There's more.

—More?

—Yes.

—What else? Homer asked.

Ezra explained to his father that there was another child involved, one whom Homer and Isabel had yet to meet; one who was of their flesh and blood and stock.

—With Dorothy?

—With Olga, Ezra told his father.

—Olga?

Ezra explained who Olga was; she was their friend in Sant'Ambrogio in the foothills up above Rapallo. Ezra and Dorothy were living in Olga's house, and so was Olga.

—You had a baby, a child, with Ol, Olg—

—Olga, Ezra said. Yes, I did.

—When? his father wanted to know.

EP. Some time ago.
Molti anni fa.

HOMER. *Molti anni…*
How long ago?

EP. The child is almost grown.
She's sixteen or so.
Lives in the north.
In the mountains.
Was raised by peasants.
She has only now
Been informed
Of all the relationships
And the patrimony.

HOMER. What kind of patrimony
Can you give someone
Who didn't even know
That you were her father?

EP. I don't know, Dad.
But she wants to meet you and Mom.

HOMER. Her name?

EP. Her name?

HOMER. Yes.
She has a name, this child.
What is it?

EP. Mary.

HOMER. Mary.

EP. She's lovely, Dad.

HOMER. When can we meet her?

EP. Soon.

HOMER. I'm not going to be around
Much longer, Ezra.

EP. Very soon, Dad.

(Isabel enters with tea tray)

ISABEL. Tea.
Now what have you boys
Been gabbing about,
I want to know?

CHAPTER NINE

"Chesterton's England of has-been and why-not,
or is it all rust, ruin, death duties and mortgages
and the great carriage yard empty
and more pictures gone to pay taxes"
—"Canto LXXX"

1.

Outside the window, Paris. Inside the room, a table at which T. S. Eliot and Ezra Pound were sat, editing Eliot's poetry. Eliot had the look of a proper Englishman, a pin-striped suit, polished brogues on his feet, a proper shirt and tie. The only thing that betrayed that look was his accent, a combination of the Midwest and High Church English, an accent not really spoken by anyone in St. Louis or London. A linguist might call it Midlantic, somewhere between high English and proper American speech. In Eliot's case, it was totally fabricated, the cadence and rhythms invented wholecloth. EP's speech was equally canned. He spoke sometimes like a cowboy, sometimes like a bardic shaman; his speech was even more invented than Eliot's, and had notes of Philadelphia, that annoying way they said "roof," for instance, almost as obvious as a Canadian saying "about." Ezra also had that High English accent that drifted in and out of his speech, plus he liked to pepper his conversations with French, Provençal, Italian, Latin, and sometimes a bit of Greek and even, lately, some Mandarin Chinese, just to keep everyone honest. As to his haberdashery and his kit, he wore something more bohemian, sneakers, corduroy trousers, a thick knitted jumper, and a huge red scarf tied in a hangman's knot around his neck, plus a floppy oversized beret on his head, cut at a rakish angle. Yes, he wore a beret, something that just wasn't done in Paris. He had a mad gleam in his eye, as he was so very pleased with what he had been reading on the page. Pound said: I have finally met someone who I believe is smarter than I am.

—Who is that, Mr. Pound?

Ezra scratched his beard.

—You, he said.

—Me?

—Yes, you.

Eliot paused.

He looked out the window at the Parisian rooftops.

—I'm flattered.

Mr. Eliot seemed almost deflated of any emotion, a true Englishman, only he was from St. Louis, Missouri, a Yank, through and through. Where Pound was all energy and excitement, Eliot appeared neurasthenic, wary and unenergetic; he wore pinstripes, and had on a tie, and brogues on his feet that looked as if they weighed a ton. He sipped a whiskey; Pound drank beer from the bottle, and occasionally snorted something up his nose, though he would not reveal what it was.

Tom Eliot thought that perhaps Ezra Pound was taking the piss, putting him on, with the sniffing of whatever it was he sniffed.

—Don't be flattered, Pound said. There's no need for false modesty here. There is real genius in your poems.

—No one's ever said that, Eliot pronounced, nonplussed.

—Well, I'm saying, Pound shouted. But it needs a lot of editing. That's why I'm here. I'm going to edit it for you.

—Such as?

—Top to bottom, Pound declared. Nose to tail.

Eliot didn't seem to understand, but Pound assured him that he did not have to understand. After all, he was the poet. He only had to write the poems. Others would edit them (Pound) or write about them, admiringly (the rest of the world).

—What you need to do is give me permission, Ezra said.

—To do what, Mr. Pound?

Ezra stood up and walked around the room. He walked like an athlete, maybe a tennis player. He had a good stride. Energy poured out of him. He seemed as if he never ran out of gas. He smiled. He scratched his messy head of hair. He laughed.

—Why, to edit this mess you have given me.

Eliot said that he was rather fond of some of the poems. He said that he would not call them a mess. But Pound explained his position. He said that Eliot's poems were very good, but that their very goodness was what was preventing them from becoming—from being—great. He said to Mr. Eliot that he, Ezra Pound, wanted to edit his poems to make them excellent.

—I don't want to edit them just to get them published, he said, laughing maniacally. The laughter somewhat threw off Tom Eliot. What was this man saying? Pound said that he wanted the poems to be the bellwether of new sensibil-

ity, of this age, "the Modern Age," he called it. Thus Ezra
Pound to T. S. Eliot.

—The Modern Age?

2.

—There is Modernism in art,
With Picasso and Braque,
Picabia and Matisse.
There is Modernism in music,
With Stravinsky and others.
We now need Modernism
In poetry, to not so much
Cauterize the old from our poems,
But to make what is worth saving
Into a new way of expressing
Ourselves to the contemporary world,
But also to posterity,
So that people fifty years
From now will be discussing
Your poetry as if it had just been written.

3.

Eliot had to think about what his new friend Ezra Pound
was saying. He had great ambitions for his poetry, he said.
Don't get me wrong, Mr. Pound. But I am not sure that I
see it having the effect you describe. Pound banged his fist
on the wooden table top. No, no, no! he shouted. You are

quite and unequivocally wrong, Tom. You are potentially the greatest writer of the 20th century. You in poetry; Joyce in prose.

—I am not sure I would agree with that estimate, Mr. Pound.

—Call me Ezra.

—Ezra.

—What shall I call you?

—Possum.

Pound laughed. Not only did he laugh, he guffawed. He threw his head back, stomped his feet, and let out a loud yodeling howl.

—Possum? he said.

—Yes, you can call me Possum, Eliot told him without losing a beat or appearing one bit ruffled by the conversation.

—All right...Possum.

—That's fine, Eliot declared, as if a great burden had been lifted from his narrow shoulders. Eliot metaphorically rolled up his sleeves, even put on a green visor, and took out his blue pencils.

—Now tell me here what you have in mind, he said.

4.

EP. I want to edit out sixty to eighty percent
Of what you have written here,
Keeping what works,
And merging it all into a new work.

ELIOT. What will I call it?

EP. With these particular poems,
I was thinking of calling it
"The Waste Land."

ELIOT. "The Waste Land?"

EP. It will be the poem
That makes the world
Recognize
Your genius.

ELIOT. You are so self-confident, Ezra.

EP. I'm very smart, Possum.

ELIOT. You are.

EP. There is only two people smarter
Than I am.

ELIOT. Who are they?

EP. You and Jimmy Joyce.

5.

Joyce was clever, no doubt about it. But Eliot found Joyce to be a bit too disingenuous. His politeness was a kind of masque, which Eliot could forgive and even admire were Joyce an Englishman. But somehow an Irishman behaving in that superior manner was disconcerting. And yet, like Pound, Eliot saw the genius in the writing. What it was that Eliot liked the writing enormously, but he did not necessarily care that much for the man, his frailty, his narrow, tall frame, his banker suits, his patchy eyes. But these thoughts were only velleities, weak and unformed. There was so much pride on display in Joyce's public demeanor, thought Eliot, and yet Joyce was good enough a fellow as far as Eliot was concerned.

6.

EP. He's a genius.
Just like yourself.

ELIOT. I do like his writing.

EP. You both understand mythology,
Both know how to use it
In the contemporary world,
Incorporating it
Into your philosophies.

ELIOT. I am humbled
By your assertion, Ezra.
You are the inventor
Of Chinese poetry
For our time.

EP. You are the inventor
Of Modern poetry,
Possum, Mr. Eliot,
Poor Tom.

ELIOT. I shall always be
Indebted to you,
Ezra.

EP. You will be the spine
Of American poetry,
From now until the end
Of time.

ELIOT. Time past
And time present:
To be present
For your life…

EP. This may be
The most spiritual thing
Any one of us
Are able to
Do in his short life.

ELIOT. What's past is past,
Until it becomes the present.

EP. The present is all
We have.

ELIOT. And our friendship,
Which is both past and present,
Is present and future.

EP. Future perfect.

7.

But there were other important matters to discuss. Pound looked very seriously at his new friend. Now tell me about these cats you saw, he said. They were everywhere, Eliot, Possum, told him. I put out plates of milk for them, Pound said. For them to drink. The cats. Ah, the cats, Eliot said. Yes, the cats, Pound answered. You put out the plates of milk for the cats to drink? Eliot asked.

Was that not clever of me? Pound said. You are a most clever fellow, Eliot answered. We must go together some night, bringing a bottle of milk for them. To feed the cats? Eliot asked. Yes, Pound said, to feed. The cats. The cats. In a word...

8.

And where was Yeats in all this? He was off with the fairies, Pound said. He's always there with them. He believes in them? Eliot asked. Yes, he does, Pound said. He believes wholeheartedly in the fairies. And what else? Eliot asked. Yeats believes in all manner of things, Ezra told Possum. Such as? Such as ghosts, spirits, parallel universes, wormholes in the universe through which we tread to another world. He's daft. But a good poet, Eliot said. Pardon me for saying this so bluntly, Eliot, but Yeats is the greatest poet in the English language. According to? According to Pound himself—myself! Ah, Eliot said. *Ex cathedra* from Pound himself. In a manner of speaking, Pound said. In a manner of speaking, Eliot repeated. And where is Yeats now? Eliot asked. He's feeding cats. Where? In Rapallo. Downtown. Near my parents' house. Shall we join him? asked poor Tom. We shall, Ezra said. Let me find some milk. We need a bottle of milk and some fishy bits. Fishy bits, Eliot said, savoring the idea. He could almost taste the salt of the fish on his tongue. Such was the power of the imagination, he thought, sometimes more powerful than the senses themselves. Sometimes more powerful than anything on earth. Perhaps Yeats was right, Eliot thought. The spirits were everywhere. We had to appease and honor them. We had to go to them to find our words.

CHAPTER TEN

"Behold me, Vidal, that was fool of fools!
Swift as the king wolf was I and as strong
When tall stags fled me through the alder brakes,
And every jongleur knew me in his song,
And the hounds fled and the deer fled
And none fled over long."
        —"Piere Vidal Old"

Olga lived in the hills above Rapallo in a little house in Sant'Ambrogio. During the war, Ezra showed up with his wife Dorothy, so that the three of them all lived together in regular disharmonious marital bliss. Olga said that they were all civilized people, so that it would be possible, and Dorothy didn't have a leg to stand on once she told Ezra that their son Omar was not from Ezra's loins, not his patrimony. Dorothy had met an Egyptian man in her travels and they had an affair. It did not last long. But it did produce Omar. Ezra had his own bundle of joy, Mary, living far north of Rapallo, with some local farmers, people whom Olga picked out as being reliable and trustworthy and able to raise a child. She provided them with some money. Dorothy laughed remembering that Olga had asked her to cook when she first arrived from down below in Rapallo because Dorothy had never cooked a thing in her life. I am not that kind of person, Dorothy said. Well, what kind of person are you? Olga asked. We are Shakespears, Dorothy said, as if that explained everything. Well, I play music, I'm a musician, Olga told her. I am not often around to cook and tidy up. I am not going to cook for you and Ezra, Dorothy declared. We shall be just three people living in the hills above Rapallo, with Ezra's parents down below in the town in that apartment he found for them before the war forced us up into the hills to live with Ezra's—

Suddenly words were lost in Dorothy's mind.

—Concubine, Olga said.

—Yes, Dorothy said. I mean, no.

Ezra was the least concerned of everyone about the arrangement. He looked at it as being a good set-up, as he could be with his wife Dorothy and the woman he loved, who was Olga.

They all knew it was because of the war, which had made things different in every way. The war had put the three of them together. Before the war, Dorothy and Ezra had lived in Rapallo, not far from his parents, and Ezra would spend part of every week up in Sant'Ambrogio with Olga. His parents were old and retired and he was concerned about them, so he would leave the hills and venture back down the trail into Rapallo to visit his parents and then spend a few days with Dorothy, his wife. Ezra would sometimes daily climb the hill, taking the *salita*, up into and beyond Sant'Ambrogio, visiting Olga by daylight, bringing her things from town. He would read to her; they would eat together or just sit in each other's company, enjoying the peace or the music they listened to on the Victrola. He would write there and she composed music. They had been seeing each other since 1925, so the arrangement stood in place a long time. It was nearly twenty years they had known one another.

Olga reminded Ezra not to forget their daughter.

—Our daughter, he said.

—Mary.

—Mary.

Omar, Dorothy's son, was in England. Her son, he now said, disavowing any connection to the boy.

—He has your last name, Dorothy reminded her husband.

But there was no blood between them. Mary at least was his daughter.

—Mary, Mary, quite...

He sang the nursery rhyme, smiling.

—My Egyptian lover, Dorothy said, just to put him on notice, to irritate the shit out of him. Two can play this game, Ezra.

—EP and I have each other.

—And Mary.

—And Mary, Ezra said.

—Mary, Mary, quite...he sang.

Dorothy spoke to herself in a corner of the little house. She said that Ezra was not seemingly able to have a child with her, but that she managed to get pregnant with the Egyptian lover. Ezra complained that there was nowhere to do work with children everywhere. So Dorothy, to appease him, sent Omar to England to be raised and educated. Her own family was still there, substantial and able to care for Omar.

And Olga gave Mary to the peasant couple in the Italian Alps.

—In the Alps, Ezra repeated.

—In the Alps, said Olga.

Eventually Olga told Mary who her real parents were. Her mother was a classically trained musician, highly successful in what she did. Her father was the renowned poet and writer Ezra Pound.

Olga had wanted a boy, a son, but it was Dorothy who had the son with her Egyptian lover.

—It was so Coptic, Ezra said.

He had told Olga that the marriage was a sham, but that he would not leave Dorothy because of her parents, and Dorothy and Ezra had been so much together. It was hard to erase all that. The London years. The Paris years. The years in Rapallo. She was a Shakespear. Eliot and Joyce knew them as a couple. They were all friends. Eliot and Joyce, the two great geniuses of the 20th century, they were their friends. They had drunk tea and whiskey with them, drank wine and smoked cigarettes or let them smoke and watched the gray smoke curl through their hands and waft skyward to the ceiling. It was almost as if they were mortals.

—Ezra wore green trousers in London, Dorothy said, to no one particularly. He had had them made from billiard table felt. And he wore a pink shirt. He had one turquoise earing.

If Ezra were to jettison her, there would be no other person to remember these things. It would almost be as if they had never happened. Dorothy remembered him in his various capes. His slouch hat. He was nothing if not theatrical. There was no one quite like Ezra Pound in those days in London. He was brilliant and full of opinions. His energy was protean. He had the soul of a poet, bursting with words, ideas, notions, rhythms he needed to get down on the page. There was no one quite like him, thought Dorothy. He would shout out in the middle of a room: Poetry is news that stays news. Half the time no one knew what he was banging on about, although there were always a few cognoscenti who understood that he was a kind of oracle. His ideas shocked London at the turn of the century and I loved him for that.

But Ezra never saw the marriage as anything other than a convenience. Eliot had his marriage of inconvenience. Joyce had his non-marriage of cohabitation with Nora Barnacle; they had their children, and they were a family. Dorothy called it a marriage of minds, but Olga said to Ezra that she did not think that it ever was a marriage of minds. Olga said: I don't think Ezra ever loved Dorothy the way he loved me.

—She knew nothing about me, Dorothy said, laughing.

Ezra met Olga at a concert. She was performing. He was into the music and poetry of the troubadours.

—Ezra loved Jimmy Joyce. He loved Hemingway, Dorothy said. He loved Eliot. Possum, he called him. He and Ezra were like brothers, like Dante and Cavalcanti, only they never could decide who was who. Ezra said that Possum was Cavalcanti and that he was Dante. *Il miglior fabbro.* The finer craftsman. What Possum called Ez.

One day while Dorothy was outside smoking a cigarette

or staring at the garden out back, Ezra asked Olga, Where's Mary? In the Alps, Olga said. Olga explained to Ezra her reasoning. Mary was not refined enough. She was rough at the edges. She lacked sophistication or even an education, in music and the arts and literature. She's bright enough, Pound said, even though he hadn't seen her in years. She has dirt under her fingernails, Olga said, laughing. There were weeds in her hair. Olga wanted to introduce Mary to society, to present her at the music festivals that she performed at every year in Siena.

—We both loved Ezra, Dorothy said to a stray cat, and hated each other.

The cat stopped and stared at Dorothy for a moment, then sauntered away.

The Nazis had cleared everyone from the waterfront in Rapallo, so Olga had to take Ezra and Dorothy in. They had nowhere to go. You couldn't leave them in the cold. Not Ezra. Not even Dorothy. It was not done. Olga detested Dorothy, but then again Dorothy returned the favor, detesting Olga, who was a thorn in Dorothy's heart. Olga had six rooms in the hills up from Rapallo, away from the sea where the Nazis waited for the Americans to come to the shore.

They all knew, the three of them, what the Americans were saying, that they wanted to indict Ezra or maybe already had. They wanted to try him for treason, only Ezra never believed the rumor. He did not believe he had done anything wrong by broadcasting for the Axis powers during the war years.

—I NEVER SD
OR DID
  ANYTHING

AG'INST MY CONSCIENCE

Thus spake King Ezra. He would do nothing, he said many times, against his own nature, as an American, or against nature itself. He had his ideals.

John Adams
Jefferson
Mussolini...

Olga would say that they had all once lived separately and well, and they were civilized. Dorothy agreed: they were civilized. But Olga said that Dorothy treated her like a maid, even though they were staying in Olga's own house. But Dorothy was discreet. If they were doing something—anything—she kept to her own room. But cooking/cleaning, Olga endured Dorothy for a year. Dorothy called it her hell, up that *salita*, up that hill, in Olga's house. Sant'Ambrogio. Ezra ignored the circumstances or, more accurately, was totally unaware of them. He wrote his books, his articles, his poems. The long poems, *The Cantos*, moved ever onward. Besides his poetry, he read his books on economics and, in turn, wrote his books about economics too. He worked for the broadcasting radio network in Rome. For the Fascists. For the Boss. Benito himself. Muss, Ezra called him. Yet the world each day got smaller and more dangerous. The Allies closing in. The Axis shutting down. The end nigh.

There was no water in the house.

—There was water, Olga said.

—No water, Dorothy claimed. None in the dry season. No heat in winter. A perpetual struggle for wood, for food, for survival.

One day, after coming back from Rome, Ezra said, In the distance, over the mountains, you heard Genoa being destroyed by the Allied bombardments, even Rapallo, the church, the railroad bridge, all destroyed. The main plaza in Rapallo, destroyed, by the bombs.

—Now the Fascists wanted Ezra to do broadcasts in Milan, Olga said.

—He's sixty years old, Dorothy said. He's losing his strength. He cannot do what he once was able so easily to accomplish.

Ezra found the isolation instructive. He read Confucius. He thought. He wrote. But Olga could not play her music. It was too hard to do, given the circumstances.

—Because of her in my house, Olga said.

—Because of the bombs, Dorothy said.

EP. I would think,
And I would write,
Until there was
Nothing,
    Nothing
To think,
Nothing
To write.

DOROTHY. I was silent.

OLGA. I had nothing to say.

EP. I said nothing.
I said nothing
About the Jews,
　Nothing

About the world
Conspiracies,
The world
Collapsing
Around us.
I was silent
About the Jews,

About the world
Collapsing.

Chapter Eleven

Atennis court in Paris. Ernest Hemingway and Ezra Pound arrive at the court. Hemingway wears sweat pants and sweat shirt and sneakers. Pound wears his usual flamboyant garb. He carries two tennis rackets and balls, while Hemingway caries hand wraps and large, puffy 16-ounce sparring gloves to teach Ezra the poet about boxing. Pound's two concessions to tennis-play are a pair of white plimsolls and a cottony bucket hat daringly placed upon his head. Hemingway explains the hand wraps and the gloves to his poetry friend and fellow ex-pat American. Without them, he says, holding up the wraps and the gloves, you would break your hands. You'd break your fuckin' hand, Ezra. Do you understand what I am saying? D'accords, Pound said, anxious to get started, tennis or boxing, it did not matter to him. And yet he finally said, remembering why they had come to the courts:

—I thought we were going to play tennis, Pound said.

—We'll play tennis, then do some sparring.

—Where?

—Right here on the court.

—What if someone comes along?

—Fuck 'em, Hemingway said. We're Americans. They'll think we don't know what we are doing. They'll be right.

—I like the way you think, Hem. But do me a favor.

—What Ez?

—When you write…

—When I write?

—Yes, I am speaking about your prose, Hem.

—My prose?

But then the conversation did not so much stop as gone on hiatus.

They walked out on the court, rackets in hand. They warmed up, then began to play. Pound was clearly the better tennis player. Hemingway seemed more raw in his talents, occasionally hitting a zinger, but mostly bageling the returns. Ezra had an elemental stroke; his serve was clean and efficient. When the ball landed on the clay court, it had some spin on it. Hemingway never sure which way the ball was going to drift.

Ezra returned a backhand, then volleyed with Ernest.

Pound won the point.

The two Americans played several games of tennis, all of which were won by Ezra Pound. Then Ernest Hemingway suggested that he give Ezra another kind of lesson. He picked up the hand wraps, first wrapping his friend's hands, then his own. They put on these big, bulky 16-ounce leather boxing gloves, no headgear and no mouthpieces, and stood facing each other in the middle of the tennis court in Paris.

Hemingway worked hard to show Pound what he was doing wrong. His balance was wrong. His stance was wrong. His feet were in the wrong place; they were too far apart. They should only be the length of one's shoulders, Hemingway said. But Ezra was a quick study and a good student. Soon he had his left foot pointing towards Ernest. When Hemingway shoved Pound the poet did not budge, his balance being that good almost immediately. They circled one another. Hemingway jabbed and Pound slipped and slid away from the jabs. Ezra threw a dynamic right cross but Ernest slipped it easily. He said that Pound was telegraphing his punches. He said that Pound did not understand how to jab.

—You set up all your fucking punches, your combinations, off the jab, Hemingway shouted, even though Pound was only steps away.

Hemingway put together a five-punch combination—the jab, two punches to either side of Ez's body, and then two head shots, one on each side of his face. Ezra, being slightly crazy, was game, and he laughed and danced away from Hemingway's punches. This seemed to infuriate the prose writer momentarily until he settled down and began to jab at his friend's poetic face.

Pound, in turn, though only a novice, slid underneath a punch and landed one on Hemingway's jaw that made him dizzy for one moment. But the poet then would have to pay the price for such an infraction. Hemingway battered Pound from pillow to post, sending him backpedaling around the tennis court.

A group of Parisians had gathered now, watching the two Americans batter each other in the improvised boxing ring. We were far from David's painting of the tennis-court oath. This was the raw energy of American writers willing to bloody each other to prove, what, their courage and masculinity?

Finally Pound was the first one to throw in the towel. He had had enough. Exhausted, they sat down on a bench at the end of the tennis court. Pound drank some water; Hemingway had brought along some bottles of beer, one of which he uncorked and drank from. Ezra wanted to return to something he had tried to tell Ernesto when they had first arrived at the court. It was the matter of his prose, Ezra thought. It was the matter of his style. There was nothing more important than prose and style, he told his American friend. Poetry ought to be at least as well written as prose.

EP. When you write,
Use fewer words.
Be exact.

EH. Exact?

EP. Don't waste the words.
Look for *le mot juste.*

EH. Flaubert!

EP. *Exactement*!

—And direct treatment of the object, Pound shouted.

—Example, Hemingway said, in a clipped, almost militant way.

EP. Don't call a sunrise
A gilded dome of light.

Or a bird
A flying angel.

And if you know
The name

Of the bird
(A sparrow or hawk or nightingale)

Call it by its name.
Comprends?

EH. *Je le comprends bien*, Ez.

EP. Write out of
The rhythm
Of experience.

—I am, Hemingway said, and then squished his gloved left hand into Pound's nose with a stiff jab.
—Good, Pound said.
But it was unclear if he meant the jab or the remark his prosewriting American friend had just said.
—It is good, Hemingway said.
—What? Pound asked. The punch or the line.
Hemingway laughed.
—Give me some more advice, Ez.

EP. Don't write
By the metronome.

EH. But do write
By the rhythms
Of the Metro.

EP. *Certainement.*

EH. Let's have a drink.

When they stopped sparring, they went to a café, sudorous and tired. Hemingway was talking about some fighter he knew in America, and Pound shouted—

—Stinkin' Amurka!

Hemingway ordered a beer and Ezra ordered a coffee.

—I like the way you think, Hem.

Pound noted that since he met Hemingway that morning, his friend had consumed four or five bottles of beer, some at the tennis court and now in the café. Ezra was not a big drinker; in fact, he could take it or leave it most of the time. He liked a good wine at the meal. That was about it. He had never acquired an abiding taste for liquor, the gins, the vodkas, the whiskeys of the world.

It began to rain all over Paris.

The two sat in their seats at the café, watching the rain fall.

Pound thought of a line of French poetry about the rain falling like the rain falling in his heart. He couldn't remember the line's author, though. It was one of those quirks of the mind, that even a person with an encyclopedic knowledge of all poetry would have this minor glitch in the mind. So he decided to forget about who wrote the line about the rain falling outside and in one's heart. Instead he said:

—So Hem, how did I do?

Hemingway stared off towards the urban landscape's

horizon. He had what combat soldiers call the thousand-yard stare, a symptom of all (usually foot) soldiers who have been involved in a shit storm somewhere. He was like that for a good minute or two, then he came back to Paris, the table, the café, and his friend Ezra Pound. He looked over at Pound who was bouncing around in his chair, still full of energy.

—Pound for pound, he said, you are the best in your weight class. Pound for pound, you might be the best around. Don't let your fucking crazy American prejudices—your crazy American politics—fuck it up, Ezra.

—Pound for pound, Pound said. I like that. May I use it?

Hemingway ignored the question and repeated:

—Don't fuck it up!

Pound did not ask what "it" was, but he presumed that Hemingway meant his career, his life, his talents, his position in the literary community as an editor and writer.

—Pound for pound, Ezra repeated. I like it.

And again, he asked:

—May I use it?

Hemingway was back to staring at the horizon and did not seem to be present at the café table and yet he was still able to say, almost like Jimmy Joyce's Molly Bloom—

—Yes…

CHAPTER TWELVE

"And Thseng-sie desired to know:
'Which had answered correctly?'
And Kung said, 'They have all answered correctly,
'That is to say each in his nature.'"
—"Canto XIII"

1.

The lecturer and poet Dermot Froidveaux stood in front of his graduate creative writing seminar at New York University (NYU). It was autumn in New York, a beautiful crisp day in October, in fact, the feast of St. Francis of Assisi. Usually Dermot took his wife and daughters to St. John the Divine Church on Amsterdam Avenue near 112th Street, up by Columbia University, to watch the blessing of the animals. But today he had to teach a seminar. The windows of his classroom on University Place were open wide, the cool autumn breeze rolling through the late afternoon of the room. He was coming to the end of whatever it was he was talking about, which happened to be a poetry session. Dermot was a tall, slim fellow with bushy black curly hair and a beard. He wore jeans and chambray shirt and had on a pair of Converse high-top black sneakers and wore a dark green corduroy jacket which had seen better days, and yet it still remained his favorite apparel. He wore black reading glasses the better to appraise the poem in the book he held in his hand. His speech was Midlantic, neither Irish, from whence he came, nor American, where he was. There was a bit of New York in his speech from his years in that city. There was a bit of Dublin, still, once in a while, especially on the "th" words that invariably became "t" words. Instead of thinking, he taught, he said, or instead of thank you, it was t'anks. Each year he looked forward to discussing Ezra Pound, his favorite poet, well, not really his favorite, probably Yeats had that honor, but the poet Dermot spent most time deciphering and, if not defending—most of Pound's politics were indefensible—then at least Dermot could elucidate the poetry, whose value was still great, in terms of influence, in terms of originality, in terms of breadth of knowledge, in terms of being the nexus of all things Modern.

—So we've been talking
About Pound's ideas concerning verse
And how to write it.
He believed in the direct treatment
Of the object.
Concision. *Le mot juste.*
The right word. He believed that poetry,
To be good, ought to be at least as well
Written as prose. He also believed
That we should avoid writing
by the metronome, da-dah, da-dah,
Da-dah, da-dah, da-dah,
And we should be writing
Out of the rhythm
Of experience.

2.

The class sat around an oblong table, the lights were off because it was still Daylight Savings Time, which would end that weekend. He could hear the noise of the street below. The streets of New York never failed to interest Dermot. In many respects, he was the opposite of Ezra Pound, who was strictly focused on Europe, with his longish dips into Confucius. Dermot did his doctorate at Oxford, in American studies, a relatively new Oxonian field, and he had written about Pound and Williams' influence upon the American alternative writers from the late 1950s and early 1960s, ranging from Frank O'Hara and John Ashbery and the other so-called New York School poets, and ranging down through Creeley and Olson and the Black Mountain poets, and out to San Francisco and Robert Duncan and especially Jack Spicer. There were many others, and he had read them all, as well as his own countrymen and women. The Irish women poets were taking hold; they were making a dent in the male façade of Irish poetry, and he felt that it was about time and that justice was being done.

A student waved his hand in front of Dermot, who stood at the front of the long oblong table.

—His poems are really hard to understand.

This was not one of his best students. In fact, he wondered how this student had gotten into New York University's graduate creative writing program. The student seemed like a lawyer, one of those lawyers who thinks he's literary, arguing that De Vere, not Shakespeare, wrote the major plays in the canon.

Another student spoke up without raising her hand.

—Yeah, he writes in Greek and Chinese, what the fuck!!??

Like the young man who preceded her, Dermot did not see a future in writing for this one. She seemed like a future lawyer too.

—We'll get to that. Let's start with something else, though. I asked you to read Chapter One, in the *ABC of Reading*.

—The fish story! a third student shouted.

The class laughed.

—Agassiz asked a student to describe a fish. It was a sunfish, the student said. "Write a description of it," Agassiz said.

The fourth student asked: Are we ever going to get to read our own poems in this class?

—Patience, Dermot said.

—It's been several weeks, that fourth student declared.

Dermot went on without responding to that student.

—The student came back and described the Ichthus Heliodiplodokus, the sunfish. Once again Agassiz told the student to describe the fish. The student produced a four-page essay. Look at the fish, Agassiz said. The student looked.

The fourth student said: Is this going to be much longer?

—After three weeks, the fish was in an advanced state of decomposition. But the student had learned quite a bit about the sunfish.

The first student who had spoken earlier in the class said that she had a poem to read.

—This is a writing workshop, isn't it?

—We'll get to that. Who has read the poem entitled "Canto XXXVI"?

Half the class raised their hands.

—That should be 100% of you. This is an advanced class. Let's take it from the top.

3.

"A lady asks me
I speak in season
She seeks reason for an affect, wild often
That is so proud he hath Love for a name."

Now we had read his Canto about usury,
About money lending illegally,
And we have read his poems from *Cathay*,
Including "The Seafarer." But what
Is he doing in this poem?

STUDENT 2. It's a love poem.

DERMOT. Yes, it would seem to be a love poem.
Anything else that you were able to find out?

STUDENT 3. Isn't this a translation
Or at least a loose translation
Of an older poem?

STUDENT 1. Cavalcanti.

DERMOT. Yes, Cavalcanti.

Remember I told you that Pound
Was a sublime linguist.
He knew many Romance languages,
Including ones that we no longer use,
Such as poems from the Provençal.

STUDENT 2. Who is Cavalcanti?

4.

Dermot explained. Cavalcanti was a friend of Dante's.

—In fact, I would like to read you a sonnet which Dante
wrote about Guido and another friend named Lapo. You
see Cavalcanti was as famous as Dante, if not more so, and
some even thought that he was a better poet than Dante.
Of course, I would disagree, and I think T. S. Eliot would
disagree, and maybe even Guido and Lapo would disagree
with that assessment.

A student asked him to read the poem. Dermot explained to the class that the sonnet by Dante, concerning
his friendship with Guido and Lapo, was his favorite poem
of all time. He read:

"Guido, vorrei che tu e Lapo ed io
Fossimo presi per incantamento,
E messi ad un vascel, ch'ad ogni vento
Per mare andasse a voler vostro e mio."

STUDENT 4. Translation.

DERMOT. "Guido, I wish that you and Lapo and I

Could be taken as if by enchantment,
And put on a boat, that with each wind,
It might sail the sea at your wish and mine."

STUDENT 1. That's beautiful.
Both in Italian and in translation.
In its original, it's pure sound,
It's pure poetry.

DERMOT. *Perfetto*! It's pure poetry,
Its sound being its meaning.
You get something from the poem,
Even without knowing a word
Of Italian.

5.

But that fourth students, the most difficult one in the class was lost. Another student told him to let go. Let the poem wash over you, she said. This fourth student was nearly always difficult and said.

—You let the poem wash over you. I don't understand it.

Another student offered this:

—I was confused at first, but I'm beginning to understand what Dermot has been trying to teach us about poetry.

A student who hadn't said anything aloud in weeks suddenly spoke up.

—With usura has no man a house of good stone
each block cut smooth and well fitting
that design might cover their face...

6.

STUDENT 6. With usura
hath no man a painted paradise on his church wall
harpes et luz
or where virgin receiveth message
and halo projects from incision…

STUDENT 7. With usura
seeth no man Gonzaga his heirs and his concubines
no picture is made to endure nor to live with

STUDENT 8. With usura, sin against nature,
is thy bread ever more of stale rags
is thy bread dry as paper,
with no mountain wheat, no strong flour…

STUDENT 3. That's so cool.
When did you guys come up with that?

STUDENT 7. That's "Canto XLV," about usury.

STUDENT 8. Pound was an Imagist.

STUDENT 6. And a Vorticist.
He was very Modernist in his ideas.

7.

Dermot looked very pleased with his graduate seminar.
He said: Ezra Pound was the prism through which Mod-

ernism passed. Some people believe that Pound invented it, Modernism, and at least every Modernist had this one thing in common, that nearly every one of them had been touched by Ezra Pound, including William Butler Yeats, the greatest Irish poet of all time, and some might argue, the greatest poet writing in the English language ever.

And of course
There is T. S. Eliot, whose "Waste Land,"
Was inchoate
Before Ezra Pound began to edit it
Into the work
That we know as "The Waste Land" today.

James Joyce, Wyndham Lewis, Ford Madox Ford,
Marcel Duchamp, Robert Frost,
    Ernest Hemingway,
Whom Pound told to write
More simply.

8.

STUDENT 6. But his politics sucked.
He was a Fascist pig.

DERMOT. His politics did suck.
He was on the wrong side of history.
He was a Fascist in Italy
During the Second World War,
Broadcasting his speeches
On Rome radio during the war,
And was charged with treason

After the war ended,
Though he never was tried.
He would spend twelve long years
Twelve lonely years,
Twelve foolish years,
Making amends,
    Amending his life,
A so-called madman,
Because who else but a madman
Could go against the American grain,
And support Benito Mussolini
And Adolph Hitler in the European campaign?
He spent twelve miserable years
As a mental patient
At St. Elizabeths Hospital
     In Washington, D.C.

STUDENT 6. I heard he was also anti-Semitic.

DERMOT. I'm not ignoring all that.
We are going to address all of that.

STUDENT 6. When?

DERMOT. Very soon.
But keep an open mind for now.

STUDENT 6. My grandmother
Was part of the *kindertransports*
From Germany to England
During World War II.
She lost both of her parents.

STUDENT 2. I'm so sorry.

DERMOT. Yes, I am sorry to hear that too.

STUDENT 6. And yet you want us to read
This anti-Semitic author.

DERMOT. Pound's politics were reprehensible.

STUDENT 4. Then how can we read his poems?

DERMOT. With open minds.
After all, poetry is news that stays news.
That's his poetry. That's also who
Ezra Pound was. He's news that stays news.

STUDENT 2. How are we supposed to read the Greek
and Latin, the French and Italian in his poetry?

DERMOT. And Provençal.
He was a true scholar
Of many languages,
Including Chinese,
Though some Chinese scholars
Question the veracity
Of his translations,
And look upon his work
As creative writing,
Inspired by Chinese poetry.

STUDENT 4. I don't see why we have to read this guy.

DERMOT. Keep in mind

That I'm not here
To verify your prejudices.
I'm here, as your teacher,
To challenge
Your assumptions.

STUDENT 4. But we don't want to have to verify Mr.
Ezra Pound's prejudices either.

DERMOT. Let's go back to that story about the sun fish.
Each time the teacher asks the student to describe it,
The fish keeps changing, decomposing,
It is literally in a state of decomposition,
Of deconstructing itself before our very eyes.

It's dead.
It's decomposing.

The descriptions
    Of what the fish is—
Of its fishness—
    Keep changing.

STUDENT 4. It sounds like you really admire Pound.

9.

DERMOT. What I admire is the poetry.
I abhor the politics. I hate the man's politics.
I have sympathy for him as a human being, though.
He also suffered. He was locked up in a cage
In Pisa, Italy, left out in the elements to bake
Alive in the heat and to freeze at night in the cold,

A six-foot tall man locked in a six by seven by six foot
Cage, like an animal. He was a poet, though,
He had human feelings and he suffered,
But he was able to write about that suffering
In the *Pisan Cantos*. He was supposed to be put on
Trial for treason, but then never was, and instead
He was declared insane and locked up
In St. Elizabeths Hospital. He was locked away
For twelve long years.

STUDENT 4. They should have thrown away
The key.

DERMOT. Had his lawyer gone to trial,
Pound probably would have been acquitted.
The prosecution needed two witnesses for every act
Of treason that he was charged with, and that
Was not an easy task for the prosecution to do.
Some people think he was the greatest writer
Of the 20th century, and he was also the greatest
Editor and showman, wheeler and dealer.
Some people think he invented Modernism,
That without Ezra Pound there would have been
No movement to make it all cohere.

STUDENT 4. I can't forgive him for his anti-Semitism.

10.

As he walked through Washington Square Park, Dermot Froidveaux stopped in front of the statue of Garibaldi
and thought about Ezra Pound. What was it about Pound

that drew Dermot to him? He detested Pound's politics, and found much of his so-called madness self-serving. He was cruel to his wife and his children. He was vein. There was no sense of compassion about him. Pound never shed a tear for the Jews killed during the Holocaust. And yet he had Jewish friends, from Louis Zukofsky to William Carlos Williams. What about the great Jewish musicians? Didn't he care that they were sent to the gas chambers just as aimlessly as some unknown Jew from Cracow.

Walking through the Village never changed. It was exciting when he was a fifteen year old runaway, and it was equally exciting walking westward along West 4th Street when he was nearly a middle-aged author and university professor.

He stopped at a light on Sixth Avenue and waited for the walk sign to appear.

His wife was away with their children, visiting her family outside the city.

He could go to a film downtown or he might just catch the train uptown, at Sheridan Square, and get off at 110th Street and Broadway, walking the half block to his apartment on Cathedral Parkway. No one in the neighborhood called it Cathedral Parkway, though; it was always called 110th Street. The Cathedral of St. John the Divine was only a half block west of his flat. He could take the train uptown, the Number One, and go home and write about Ezra Pound. He had been procrastinating lately. Enough had been written about EP; why did Dermot Froidveaux need to add to the torrent of words. Some hated Pound for his antisemitism. Rightly so, Dermot thought. Some loved him for his innovations.

He stepped into a familiar place near Sheridan Square, sat down on a stool at the bar, and ordered a beer. He craved a cigarette, but he hadn't really had a cigarette in years. It was that nostalgic feeling washing over him, reminding him of the old days when he would drink and smoke and stay out all night long. Dermot had been asked to write a review of Pound's *Selected Poems* that Faber & Faber had published, so he took out a notepad, and he began to write the review, recalling Pound's poems from memory.

11.

Selected Poems 1908-1969, Ezra Pound (London: Faber and Faber, 1975), paper $16.95

Reviewed by Dermot Froidveaux

200 words

Ezra Pound: great Modernist, Fascist propagandist, anti-Semite, denizen of St. Elizabeths Hospital [ed: nota: no apostrophe], legend of 20th century poetry, editor of Eliot's "Waste Land," discoverer of James Joyce, late influence of the modern W. B. Yeats, first publisher of Frost and Hemingway, among others, a few short years after his death has a new selected poems. So controversial is Pound that some will never crack open this book because of their dislike of the man and his hateful politics. We can't blame them. But if one can overcome such animosities towards the public

Ezra Pound, there is a trove of great poems therein. Pound's *magnum opus* was *The Cantos*, epic poem of obscurity, scholarship, allusiveness, and the lived life. The *Selected* has a good mix of cantos at the end, but also includes such Poundian classics as "The Seafarer," "Song of the Bowmen of Shu," and the long sequence "Hugh Selwyn Mauberley." There is much to appeal to any reader of Modernism. This assessment of his poems does not in any way condone his aberrant political behavior which, after the Second World War, landed him in prison and then eleven years in a mental hospital outside of Washington, D.C.

12.

When he was younger, Dermot used to attend writing workshops at the Poetry Project at St. Mark's Church in the Bowery. The students were mostly from the City College of New York, uptown in Harlem. They wrote poems inspired by Black Mountain and the New York School, and they would argue into the night about Ezra Pound and William Carlos Williams. Fist fights broke out over where to break the line in a poem. It was serious business, poetry. People had tattoos on their arms which read MAKE IT NEW or No Ideas But in Things, FORM IS AN EXTENSION OF CONTENT; they argued about breath and syllable, Frank O'Hara versus Charles Olson. They worshipped writers such as George Oppen and Louis Zukofsky. They attended workshops taught by Joel Oppenheimer, a Black Mountain poet who had ink under his fingernails from having been a printer. His friends read aloud from *The Dead Lecturer* by LeRoi Jones or recited Jones' other book from that time, *Preface to a Twenty Volume Suicide Note.*

Froidveaux lived in a three-room railroad flat on East 10th Street, with the requisite bathtub in the kitchen; and then proceeded to live on every street from East 1st to East 14th over his many years in the East Village. He began near Second Avenue and ended up around Avenue D in the Alphabetland of the East Village. He worked in the Eighth Street Bookshop, where the clerks also argued about Williams and Pound, Ashbery and Creeley, and no one ever agreed about anything other than the fact that Johnson was a pig and so was Nixon, and Malcolm X was right about nearly everything, including the chickens coming home to roost. People read books about Crazy Horse. They read Herman Hesse's *Siddhartha*, read books on meditation and astrology, discussed Henry Miller's prose versus Norman Mailer's. Miller was better, the clerks agreed, especially his nonfiction, which was brilliant.

People like Anais Nin and Maurice Sendak regularly came into the bookstore, and so did the doctor Oliver Sacks, usually on his motorcycle, which he parked outside on 8th Street; the good doctor would devour books, buying armsful every week. The black critic, scholar, essayist, and fiction writer Albert Murray often stopped by and talked with the night manager Conrad. Dermot argued poetry with Andrei Codrescu (Tristan Tzara's real name, by the way, though Andrei's real name was Andrei Perlmutter). The clerks got into shoving matches about Ted Berrigan and Joel Oppenheimer, about who was a better teacher and writer, though Dermot and Andrei, even with a wealth of differences, pretty much got along with one another.

Dermot had read as broadly and deeply as anyone he knew, and also attended the City College like his friends, graduating in the top of his class. Years later, he went back into the City University system and earned a masters in English at City College, then went to Yale and Oxford and later the Graduate Center on 42nd Street and wrote a doctorate about Pound and Provençal. Already he had attended Yale University in a graduate program and flunked out, mostly because of his drinking. Like the Irish-American fiction writer John O'Hara, Dermot had dreamed of attending Yale when he was younger, though once he was there, his drinking took hold, and the dream was smashed into a thousand tiny pieces. After the various graduate programs, he taught at Columbia briefly, then he wound up at New York University, and had been there for the last ten years.

13.

Dermot finished his drink, paid, and walked to Sheridan Square. There used to be a string of bookstores he would stop in, starting with the Eighth Street Bookshop where he once worked. He'd go to the Sheridan Square bookstore, too, or to the Cornelia Street bookshop back when the Village was filled with such book places. There used to be a tiny little store on West 4th Street at the mouth of Cornelia Street, where it disgorged into Sixth Avenue, heaving uptown. Dermot would visit it regularly, finding incredible jems, a small volume of letters entitled EP to LU, a correspondence between Ezra Pound and Louis Untermeyer. It was in one of these tiny bookshops that Dermot found the Hugh Kenner volume, *The Pound Era*. He loved that book, in fact, loved all of Hugh Kenner's books and, in turn, from Kenner, he came upon Guy Davenport, and got into a correspondence with him about Pound and others.

Now it was time to go uptown. He caught the Number One train uptown, and got off at 110th Street, took out some Chinese food, and went home to read some of Pound's translations from the Provençal. Dermot could hate the politics and even the man, but the poetry was sublime, at least so thought Dermot Froidveaux, a man of great and impeccable literary taste, he was glad to tell you, if you had a mind to listen to him. Otherwise, outside the classroom, he was a man of few words.

Back in his Morningside Heights neighborhood, he often sat for hours in the Hungarian Pastry Shop, drinking coffee, eating Linza torte, and contemplating Ezra Pound. He would stare off, looking in the distance. If he wrote even a paragraph that day, he was pleased. A paragraph a day added up quickly enough. Pound was just such an example, his published work comprising many thick volumes.

While the poets from his Lower East Side workshop went off to write poems, some of them becoming as famous as their mentors, Dermot wrote less poems and more essays about poetics. He was fine with that. Everyone has a place in life, he realized, and his was to teach and to talk about someone like Ezra Pound.

Pound was the Modernist who baffled Dermot the most. He was the one who discovered Joyce and who edited Eliot, the one who got the rich patrons to pony up for the poor artists and writers in his life. He was the one-man band that promoted Modernism, though he didn't necessarily call it that from his vantage in the cauldrons of London and later Paris. Then he seemed to throw in the towel and moved to Italy when his crazy ideas began to ferment in his mind. Twenty years earlier he seemed more like a Bolshy rebel than an establishment Fascist, though his friend Wyndham Lewis seemed rightward inclined and Eliot always leaned towards the established order.

Chapter Thirteen

"WITH USURA
wool comes not to market
sheep bringeth no gain with usura
Usura is a murrain, usura
Blunteth the needle in the maid's hand
And stoppeth the spinner's cunning."
          —"Canto XLV"

1.

Europe calling: Pound speaking. There he is, *il miglior fabbro*. Where was ole Ez? He started out in Rapallo, having taken a train and other forms of transportation all the way to Rome. It was the war years, the 1940s, things being scarce, including money. He rode on the rails for free, as he was a minor personality in Mussolini's world. Ez was the commentator on the radio. But his speeches were so weird that the Italian Fascists weren't sure if he might be a spy, using a kind of code to communicate with the Americans. And yet he still faithfully went to Rome and did the taping of his broadcast which is where he heard the news that the Italians were about to surrender to the Americans. He decided to turn himself in, which is what he did, not as a prisoner because he didn't think of himself as a prisoner. He was turning himself in to the American authorities as an American himself with a special knowledge about the Italians. He could be of help to the Allies when they rebuilt Italy. He could show them the ropes, explain the differences between this faction and that, this fact or that one. He was standing down in a radio station in Rome. The war was wending to a conclusion. He was one of the Fascists, although he might take umbrage with that appellation. He was a free-thinking American, a believer in the Constitution, he might say. A free spirit. A Modernist, for Crissakes! His heroes were Jefferson and Confucius. But also Mussolini. His heroes were Dante, Cavalcanti, Pere Vidal. Such an odd one, that Ezra. He spoke into the microphone:

I have nothing against the United State of Amurka.
I am a patriot. I am only against Roosevelt and the Jews,
Who have influenced him. I am against the banks.

He was threadbare, but only just. Things were hard to come by, especially in Italy, even if you had connections, even if Il Duce (the Douche Bag!) read your poems and admired you, even if his advisors thought you a spy or, worse, a conman. You spoke Italian with a Philadelphia accent. Was not that Philly accent perhaps the worst one of all American accents? Perhaps that is why he made up accents for himself, the cowboy, the Southern gentleman, the East Coast intellectual. There was no end to the masques and who he could be—and almost never was—wearing them. Personae, indeed. Or at least that's what he would have called it in the Twenties. Nowadays, it was more like ventriloquism. A sleight of hand.

Now he was *persona non grata.*

Or like that French word "personne," he was a "nobody." Wasn't that the worst blow of all, that he might be irrelevant?

I have attacked Alexander Hamilton, as what sane person would not.

Because of financial speculation, the real cause of all wars.

War is about profit, plain and simple.

I am against the money lords, such as Henry Morgenthau,

Because he is a usurer,

And usury is a crime against humanity.

The Rothchilds. Bernard Baruch, all usurers.

I should like to think that the American race in North America had some wish towards survival, he said. (I certainly didn't say it; I wasn't even there, hadn't even been born yet, for fuck's sake.)

That they wanted the United States of Tomorrow, Maestro Pound said. Ezray the X-Ray, the X-rated patriot, was going to wind up in the calaboose, if he didn't watch his tongue. Even Mr. President Roosevelt wanted Ezra Pound captured and caught, tarred and feathered, and shipped back to the United States of Postwar Dysfunction, and like Pound himself, America was a land of suburban prejudices, of excluding one group of people from their enclave, and finding themselves superior in the process. It was laughable if it wasn't so profoundly sad and alarming. Hitler almost won. The Fascists, had they a big bomb, had they

Von Braun's rockets, had they cold cash—they might have turned the tide, defeated the British and the Americans, and everyone would be speaking German and Japanese the world over, shouting Achtung! Lucky for us that that did not happen. Had Hitler kept the Jewish intellectuals on his side, maybe he would have developed the atomic bomb before anyone else. He was that close to getting a bomb. Imagine the carnage.

Ezra had traveled regularly from Rapallo south of Genoa to Rome in order to do his radio broadcasts. He considered it all part of his educational program about how to make wise the Americans. He wanted to sway Roosevelt. Ez was nothing if not slightly delusional. Poetry was everything, he said. Or it was nothing. Which he didn't say, but more and more thought. And if poetry is nothing, what is he, a poet, a sixty-year-old bag of flesh and bones that no slouch hat or cape could hide as being so frail and human. He had been fooling himself for a long time. Sometimes he even fooled others. After all, he was Ezra Pound, renowned poet, translator, literary raconteur. He was editor and Muse for some many others. Modernism, as we know it, had gone through him, his connections. Pound was the prism through which Modernism passed. If it did not touch Ezra or his ideas, it probably was not Modern but some facsimile of the new. You were nothing in the Twenties if more than a couple of degrees away from ole Ez.

2.

He ranted and raved into the overly big microphone, shouting his message across the airwaves. The problem with radio was that you didn't know if there was one or none or five million listening. So Ezra talked to himself, but out loud. Maybe the only listener was the U.S. government which wrote down his most incendiary remarks. Even Roosevelt himself wanted Ezra's head. Bring me the head of Ezra Pound, he shouted at his Secretary of State. Yes, sir, the man said, right away, sir. But he did not move. They would have to wait until the end of the war to bring Roosevelt the head of Ezra Pound, and by then Roosevelt was dead and Pound was imprisoned at St. Elizabeths Hospital. But then we get ahead of ourselves, and even in a Modernist tale such as this one, there is no advantage in showing our hand so early in the game.

How much liberty do you have?
How much do you want?

Who rules your rulers
In the Jewdeocracy?

Vell, I tell you, he is a Yid,
And about that, I do not kid.
He is a kike, and about them,
I must confess, I do not like.

His head was filled with kikes and hebes, yids and sheenies. Where did he learn such things? Maybe his mother. Maybe his father. Maybe the lads and ladies at school. His education was very white shoe and exclusive, very Philadelphia, even if he had been born in Hailey, Idaho when his paw was an assessor for the guvmint. Maybe it was the Philadelphia suburbs in which he grew up and prospered that turned him into a ranting anti-Semitic suburban lunatic. Maybe it was the cheese in Rapallo or the mushrooms around Sant'Ambrogio where his Muse, his honeypot, Olga Rudge lived. No Jew ever did anything to ruin his life in any way, so it was really a matter of a prejudice that had bloomed inside of him and now was uncontrollable. He was the prince of the Fascist paupers; he was poet in their midst, giving their shit-ass notions legitimacy. It was really horrible, this talented, once kind, once thoughtful, once brilliant man was wasting away, frittering away his life doing these asinine broadcasts, while six million Jews were dying in the concentration camps just to the north. How delusional must a poet be before you throw in the towel and say, Basta! Enough! Shut your fucking mouth, Ezra Pound. We are sick of your bullshitting crap. We are fed up with your larcenous, your treacherous, your treasonous behaviors. We are fed up and tired, yes, of your fear and ignorance. It is no longer acceptable. Shall I say it to you in Italian? Would that make it more palatable? *Non e acceptable parlare la questa via.* Or some such verbiage. But it was no use. He was still broadcasting his seeds of venom, his harvest of spite, across the air-waves, poisoning the well with such polluted and arsenic water.

3.

How much liberty do you have?
How much do you want?

Roosevelt and the Rothchilds,
Kikes and hyper-kikes and super-kikes,
And kikey kikes.

With their Jewspapers, and their Franklin Finkelstein
Roosevelt,
    Looking for their gelt,
    Their pound of flesh. Vell, enough is enough.
    An eye for an eye. How about this:

Don't start a pogrom. We don't need a pogrom,
Not some old style killing of the Jews.
Of course if somebody had a stroke of genius,
Then let's start the pogrom at the top,
With all the big wigs from the banks.
There might be something to say for that.

How much liberty do you have?
How much do you want?

4.

They had trouble finding bread in Rapallo, much less the other basics in life. There was no olive oil, at least, none that was worth its name. There were no lemons or garlic. You had to make deals with people in the foothills, subsistence farmers who could casually stop by their home and give his wife or his mistress the goods—some tomatoes, a few sardines fresh from the sea, a little wine. Ah, wine, when was the last time any of them had tasted a good wine? It had been ages, and here it was, what, 1944, the year of the Fascists, he thought, the year the war turns around and we drive the British and the Americans, the Russians and the kikes out of Western Europe. It was only moments away, this transformation. Or was it '45? He could not remember. His head was so full of *The Cantos*, and his complicated schemes to explain to the thick Americans his system of economics that would save the world. His head, like Joyce's, was filled with different languages, some dead, some alive, and a stew of possible juxtapositions.

5.

Round up the sixty kikes who started this war,
And we could sent them all to St. Helena,
As a measure of world prophylaxis,
And some hyper-kikes and some non-Jewish kikes
Along with them.

This is the head of the Ezuversity speaking to you in plain English.

I am here to express my free speech.
Thank you, Il Duce.

Jefferson and/or Mussolini.
Vy you should ask, darlink?

John Adams and Malatesta.
We are Murcans and Eye-talians.
Listen: I am here to help you
To see the light.
I am here to educate
The unruly and the ruly,
The wooly-minded
And the demented.

I am Ezra Loomis Pound, poet, economist, historian,
Gadfly Amurkan patriot and dissenter.

How much liberty do you have? How much do you want?

(There is a loud clank. A cage descends from above, surrounding Ezra Pound.)

Part Two

St. Elizabeths Hospital, Washington, D.C.

The apparition of these faces in the crowd;
Petals on a wet, black bough.
        —"In a Station of the Metro"

CHAPTER ONE

"The States have passed through a
dam'd supercilious era.
Down, Derry-down /
Oh let an old man rest."
—"Canto LXXXIII"

During the war, Roosevelt met regularly with Frank Biddle, his Attorney General. Now the president's illness, his paralysis, was setting in more and more. Mr. Biddle, the AG, had this thought that the Boss was a bit like Pinocchio, slowly turning to wood as the war grinded down to its end. When Roosevelt came into the Oval Office, his steel braces on his legs clanged like leg irons on a prisoner. Biddle swallowed the sour taste upon his tongue; the war had grounded him down to a fine powder. Sneeze and he was gone. But now that the Boss was ensconced in his chair behind the great desk, Biddle's cynical mood evaporated and he returned to the business at hand. They discussed the number of Americans in Europe who had been and still were aiding Hitler. They talked about what could be done when the war ended, even if Roosevelt were no longer there. Biddle was a good ear. The President enjoyed speaking to him. Today he wanted to know if they could indict all of these foreign Americans for treason, and the AG said that they were looking into the matter for the President. They might not be able to try them now, but when the war ended—

—I understand that the poet Ezra Pound is one of them, President Roosevelt said.

—He is.

—I want you to pursue him and the others.

—That's our plan.

—They're broadcasting over Axis microphones.

—They are, Biddle said.

—But we'll get them.

—We will, sir.

They would stop the traitors in their tracks. And bring them to book. Get them in the dock and convict them and hang them. The traitors.

—Even if I am no longer here, Roosevelt said.

—You'll be here, Biddle said.

—Even if I am no longer here, Roosevelt repeated, still more certain that the end, if not the war's end, was nigh.

FDR. Even when I am no longer here.
You will prosecute them:
Best, Anderson, that Pound character.
I want them all tried for treason.
For being traitors to their country.
I want them all executed. Do you understand?

BIDDLE. I do, sir, and we will bring them to book.

*

THE PROSECUTOR

That Ezra Pound, the defendant herein,
At Rome, Italy, and other places within the Kingdom
Of Italy, and, as hereinafter described, in the District

Of Columbia, within the jurisdiction of this court, and
At other places throughout the United States
And elsewhere, continuously, and at all times
Beginning on the 11th day of December, 1941,
And continuing thereafter to and including
The date of the presentment and filing
Of this indictment, the manner and by the means
Hereinafter set forth, then and there being
A citizen of the United States, and a person
Owing allegiance to the United States,
In violation of his said duty of allegiance,
Knowing, intentionally, willfully, unlawfully,
Feloniously, traitorously, and treasonably
Did adhere to the enemies of the United States,
To wit, the Kingdom of Italy, its counselors,
Armies, navies, secret agents, representatives,
And subjects, and the military allies
Of the said Kingdom of Italy, including
The government of Japan, with which
The United States at all times since December 11, 1941,
Have been at war, giving to the said enemies of
The United States aid and comfort within
The United States and elsewhere.

**(Lights up on a federal courtroom in Washington, D.C.
EP sits at a table with his lawyer)**

The defendant, Ezra Loomis Pound, committed
Each and every one of the covert acts
Herein described for the purpose of,
And with the intent to adhere to
And give aid and comfort to the Kingdom
Of Italy, and its military allies, enemies of

The United States, and the said defendant,
Ezra Loomis Pound, committed each
And everyone of the said overt acts
Contrary to the duty of allegiance
To the United States and to the form of
The statute and constitution in such case
Made and provided and against the peace
And dignity of the United States.

Chapter Two

"Go to the bourgeoise who is dying of her ennuis,
Go to the women in suburbs.
Go to the hideously wedded,
Go to them whose failure is concealed,
Go to the unluckily mated,
Go to the bought wife,
Go to the woman entailed."
　　　　　—"Commission"

1.

It was one of those white-shoe law firms in Washington, D.C. Dorothy Pound, the staunch, British, devoted, beleaguered wife sat rigidly in a chair in front of the large wooden desk behind which the lawyer sat. The white-shoe lawyer. Her hair was in a bun; her shoes were proper. Her clothing was frumpy. She might be considered attractive, though she was a bit stiff in her demeanor and her carriage. She was a proper Englishwoman. The doormat. The factotum. The amanuensis. The unhappy wife. Dorothy thought, well, at least he is mine again. At least that other one, that bitch from Rapallo, from San'Ambrogio, was not there to share her husband. He was all hers now, even if he was incarcerated. Even if he was incapacitated. Even if they had declared him insane. A ticker-tape flitted through her brain: What thou lovest well shall not be reft from thee. What thou lovest well is thy true heritage. Dorothy was about to become his executor, his administrator, his guardian. Nothing from that point forward could be done by Ezra alone. Any rights he once had were now relinquished. The state—his sworn enemy—had made his wife the power-of-attorney, the power to decide his every whim and need. His personhood would be surrendered to her care. She was there as her husband's guardian; she was there as the avenging angel too, the neglected, the jilted, the stilted wife, the companion who never got a thank you or acknowledgments in his dedications and in his poems. She was never his Muse, only his companion. If her name wasn't Shakespear would he ever have bothered to marry her? But now. Now. Everything had to go through his wife now. But he was locked away in Cloudcuckooland, away from the rigors and difficulties of the law. He had been deemed incompetent by reason of insanity. The case had been made by his friends and his publisher, James Laughlin. Ezra had become prematurely incompetent, unable to perform his duties, including standing trial for treason. His friends and his publisher and his attorney had decided that it was better to have him alive in a loony bin than hung from the rafters for treason; the penalty for treason was death. It was Hobson's choice. If they let him stand trial, he would spout Thomas Jefferson and Benito Mussolini, Confucius and Dante, and at the end of the day, they would have convicted him for it, and he would have been sent to the gallows. No one, other than Dorothy and James and few other friends (Eliot, Hemingway, Bill Williams) understood the choices that were being offered him, and how Dorothy had to make these decisions for Ezra because he was now deemed incompetent to do so himself.

Others made their arguments to the contrary, citing the facts of the case. There was the problem of finding two Italian witnesses who had actually observed him recording his program live in the Rome studio. The government had not been able to produce the two material witnesses. Had the publisher and the lawyer and his wife not gotten him committed, there was a good chance that the charges against Ezra would be thrown out. Still, they all felt that they had done the right thing, even if literary history might deem them to have not.

If you visited him at St. Elizabeths (no apostrophe, thank you), it seemed deeply eccentric, even weird, especially when he got off on one of his political rants. But he did not seem particularly crazy. He was surrounded by crazy people. They had become his friends and associates, and they would remain that for the next eleven years. But he was different in another way from them too. One day he would be released. They never would be.

2.

Dorothy was righteous and correct and easy to work with. She was nothing if not a bright and intelligent woman. Her upbringing was most correct; she understood the subtleties of the law and of the medical professions, including psychiatry. She knew her husband well, too, and knew that anything that was done to save his life would not be fully appreciated by him, given the circumstances. Ezra had always been a difficult person. Incarceration would only bring out further that difficulty which colored all of his choices and actions. He was loud and boastful, whereas Dorothy was quiet and demure. He was brash; she kept her own council. He was impetuous and petulant; she was considerate and reserved. He enjoyed controversy; it was his life-blood. She preferred to stand off-stage, not making waves. He was abrasive; she flowed with the situation, even with the times. But he loved his parents, and so did Dorothy. He loved language and she loved him for his language; he loved the sound of words, she loved his sounds, never the squeak of a mouse, but the roar of a lion when he declaimed his poems. They were both stylish people from a particular time, London of the Teens, Paris of the Twenties. Jazz and flappers; survivors of the Great War. Modernists, both; Futurists, even. Both had their suburban prejudices which, among themselves, they indulged, talking of Jews as the bankers and moneylenders, mostly, but sometimes they indulged other suburban prejudices, such as their narrow opinion of foreigners and black people, the smell of curry houses in London, the North African masses in Paris. They were balls of contradiction because, despite these prejudices, if asked, they both professed to love mankind. Humankind, Dorothy called it, to include women more specifically in the circle of light. Ezra was even a feminist to the general public; he believed in things that others believed in.

It was when they moved to Italy in the late 1920s and lost touch with their friends, the drumbeat of war in the European air, that their prejudices became more apparent, more obvious, and more openly spoken. There was something about raw power as expressed by Benito Mussolini that the Pounds admired.

3.

The lawyers from the white-shoe law firm liked dealing with her. Ezra might seem not their cup of tea, but a proper Englishwoman like Dorothy was a breath of fresh air in Washington.

—Are the papers drawn up? she asked.

—They are, her lawyer said.

—I'm ready to sign.

Her lawyer was young and conventionally handsome, a man of the establishment, something Ezra had fought against all his life. Yet this lawyer and his firm were keeping Ezra Pound from being executed. If they scratched below the surface, they might even find that the poet was no different than they were. He did not like the Democrats who had been in power since the 1930s, nor did this Republican Party regular, this lawyer who, though young, was already a partner in the firm. The lawyer did not like Democrats and he especially could not stand Roosevelt, and he thought that Social Security and all those other left-wing ideas from the 1930s were a bunch of hooey.

The young lawyer did not place the paperwork in front of Mrs. Pound until he had this conversation with her.

—You need to understand everything before you sign.

Dorothy looked surprised.

—I do understand, she said.

Despite her declaration, the lawyer continued.

—Your husband has been declared incompetent to stand trial because of insanity.

—I am *au fait* with everything, she said, then amended her remark, realizing that an American might not necessarily understand the concept of being *au fait*.

She paused.

—I am perfectly and properly aware of what we are doing.

Once he was satisfied that she understood, the young lawyer went ahead.

—In essence, Mr. Pound will not be able to do anything without your permission. His royalties, fees, moneys earned on the literary estate will all accrue to you.

—It may be the first time I have any control over Ezra.

Once she made that remark, Dorothy was not sure if she had actually said it aloud or had she just thought it. Certainly it had been in her mind for many years. Luckily the lawyer said that he was sorry, that he hadn't heard what Mrs. Pound had just said. Dorothy was not about to throw caution to the wind.

—Nothing.

He handed her the papers, all of which were filled with colorful pieces of paper noting where she needed to sign. This took her the better part of the next hour at the end of which the lawyer asked her:

—Is there anything else you'd like for me to discuss with you?

Dorothy paused.

—There is one other matter.

—Yes.

—When can we get him moved from St. Elizabeths to some place more comfortable?

The lawyer seemed surprised by her question. He had been under the impression that Dorothy understood everything he had been saying for the last few hours concerning her husband.

—I am not sure you understand, Mrs. Pound. That's why I want you to be certain when you sign the papers.

—Is there some problem?

How could he get her to understand?

—By having your husband declared insane, he has relinquished his rights, even his personhood. He is a kind of legal ghost. He has not been convicted of treason, and yet he also has not been acquitted of it either. We are in a legal limbo, if you will. But one thing is certain. He is not going to be executed. But in order to affect that transformation, we had to jump through several legal hoops. That involved getting your husband declared incompetent to stand trial by virtue of his being insane—mentally incompetent. He has no more rights, Mrs. Pound.

Dorothy was undeterred.

—But my rights have not been abrogated.

—No.

—And I want him moved.

The lawyer explained to her again that it was not that simple, he was afraid. It is not that easy. It can't just be done, he said, especially right now. The public would be up in arms. We need to wait. What was the problem? Dorothy asked.

—There are several problems, Mrs. Pound. Because your husband has no rights as an insane person, he has been housed at St. Elizabeths. But once he is there, it is not that easy to change the order.

Dorothy wanted to know what the young lawyer was saying.

—Most people sent to St. Elizabeths never leave it. They check in, but they don't necessarily check out.

4.

DOROTHY. You mean that they die there?

LAWYER. Yes. They die there.

(Silence)

Is there anything else you wish to discuss?

DOROTHY. Yes.

LAWYER. Go ahead.

DOROTHY. I want it understood—legally speaking—
That I am Ezra Pound's wife, and no one else is.
We have one son, and his name is Omar.
There are no other children that Ezra and I have.
Omar is the sole heir. The literary estate
Will pass on to my, to our son Omar

Upon the demise of his father, who happens
To be—legally speaking—Ezra Loomis Pound.

LAWYER. Of course, Mrs. Pound.

DOROTHY. Good.

LAWYER. That goes without saying.

DOROTHY. That Omar will inherit the copyrights,
The manuscripts, the books, the royalties, everything.

LAWYER. Certainly.

DOROTHY. No one else.

(Pause)

LAWYER. Anything else?

DOROTHY. Nothing, thank you.

CHAPTER THREE

"A lady asks me
I speak in season
She seeks reason for an affect, wild often
That is so proud he hath Love for a name"

—"Canto XXXVI"

1.

Rapallo and Sant'Ambrogio were devastated from the war. Food was still scarce, and people had no money for anything. *Dolce far niente* had been replaced by *basta cosi*. The good sweet life, doing nothing, had been replaced by *enough already.* War not only was hell; it was exhausting. The colorful world of Rapallo had become gray and unfortunate, miscreant and chaotic, a seacoast of miseries. Even easy-going Mediterranean Rapallo had stiffened and balked. Stylish people walked around the waterfront in rags, joining the traditional beggars and outsiders. A loaf of bread looked like a brick of gold. There were few cars; there was no gasoline. The greengrocer was not well stocked as it had once been. The leftists were turning in all the right-wingers, calling them Fascist bastards and wishing nothing but ill-will upon them. Neighbors who nursed grudges turned into neighbors who they did not like, claiming they were Fascists. Who was there to dispute them? There were commissions set up by the Americans and the British, stations in the hills that solicited any kind of arrant nonsense that could be classified as political information.

Dossiers were opened.

It was how the Americans were able to capture and imprison Ezra Pound; he stopped by, thinking that they would be delighted to meet him, an internationally recognized poet from the United States, a man fluent in many Romance languages. Such a being could be such a great asset to the Allies. Or so Ezra thought.

Rapallo was not the same as it had once been, a place of quiet elegance and understated luxury. The galleries and art shops were shuttered. Even the pizza parlors were closed. Even the mobsters were nowhere to be seen. The rackets had disappeared. The beautiful people of the Italian Riviera were gone, evaporated from the years of hardship during the war. Clothing shops had been replaced by men pushing carts stacked with rags. The open market was a skeleton of what it had been. But the hills around Rapallo remained green and beautiful, and Olga Rudge's place in Sant'Ambrogio remained inviting. She sat out in lawn chairs in front of her house, with her daughter Mary in the other lawn chair. Neither mother nor daughter had seen Ezra Pound since his arrest for treason. Daughter Mary asked her mother, What can we do?

2.

—Nothing, Olga said.

—Nothing? Mary asked.

—*Niente.*

—And Pound?

Oddly, that is what Mary called her father.

Olga stared out into the garden.

She took a sip of tea.

Mother explained to daughter what had happened to father. He was declared insane, Olga said. He no longer has any rights. Dorothy controls everything, and her son Omar is the only legitimate heir according to the lawyers in Washington.

—I'll be fine, Mama. But it is incredible that Babbo has been declared insane.

—It is not incredible, Olga answered. It is insane to say that one of the most brilliant people on this earth is no longer competent to write, to walk about, to wipe his own bottom without getting permission from some nurse, attendant, orderly, or doctor.

Olga took a sip from her cup.

—That is what is truly insane.

Mary, Ezra and Olga's daughter, said that her father told her, before he was arrested, that he wanted her to be his literary executor. Olga knew about that wish he had made to Olga, too, about their daughter. He had great confidence in her. But now Dorothy was his guardian. They couldn't even go to visit him at the hospital without Dorothy's permission, and so far Dorothy had not given it. Olga told her daughter that the last thing that Dorothy wanted was for Pound's real daughter to assume guardianship of his literary estate. Dorothy would have that honor now, not Olga or Mary, and Pound's wishes be damned. Mary said that if her father was back in Italy, things would be different, and

Olga agreed.

In Italy, it would be right and proper for Mary to be the executor of her father's literary estate, being his sole heir.

—He never should have been declared insane, Olga said.

3.

OLGA. Never. Had they let him
Stand trial, none of the charges
Would have stuck,
     He'd be a free man
Today,
Walking about Rapallo,
He'd be here,
At Sant'Ambrogio

Right now,
Reading to us
From his Confucian translations,

Regaling us with stories
About London
About Paris.

What they don't like
Is Ezra poking
A stick
In their eye.
That's what they don't like,
That he is ornery,
That he is alive,

That he is a poet.
That's really what
They don't like.

That he has lived his life
The way he feels like,

And he didn't give a damn what
Anyone thought.

MARY. Babbo is as sane
As the judge and the jury
And the lawyer
And all the doctors.

He's like Confucius,
Or he's like Dante,
Who was exiled
From Florence.

4.

—How long will he be incarcerated? Mary asked.

Olga hoped that it would not be too long. The charges against him were unsupportable by the evidence at hand. No one had actually seen Pound make the broadcasts, so that without two witnesses to verify his actions, no charges of treason could be brought. It was a bad idea, Olga said, to claim that Ezra was insane. Instead they should have brought him to book, put him in the dock, and had a trial. He would have exonerated himself easily. Instead Dorothy and his publisher and some of his well-meaning but misguided friends launched their claim of Ezra's insanity, and with the publisher's lawyers, they won the day. Now he was locked up for being insane, with no charges ever having been brought against him.

—He's a prisoner of conscience, Olga declared, and Mary agreed.

Her father was a prisoner of conscience.

—Hope, Olga said. We can't lose. It is all we have.

—Hope, Mary said.

—Yes, her mother agreed.

Now she picked up a light glass filled with wine and drank from it.

They had hope, mother and child, but the look on their faces did not suggest that they did. Their faces were distraught and despairing.

Mary reminded her mother that hope was the one with feathers.

Olga smiled.

5.

OLGA. I would like for you to come to my concert, darling.

MARY. I would love that, Mama.

OLGA. We need to make you
Less a farmer,
And more a civilized
Being.
More of the arts,
Concerts, galleries, books to read.

MARY. Papa has given me a list
Of all the books I need
To read before I see him again:

Jefferson, Mussolini,
Frobenius, Confucius,
Mr. Cummings,
Possum,
Mr. Joyce,
Ernest Hemingway,
Even a little bit
Of Frost.

OLGA. Only a little bit.
Frost writes with the steady beat
Of the metronome,
As your father
Would say.

MARY. Flaubert, Browning,
And Papa's own books:
Cathay, Personae,
The Cantos.

OLGA. His book on Gaudier-Brezcka.

MARY. The Odes. Cavalcanti.
Dante—

OLGA. One can never get
Too much
Dante.

The original
Il miglior fabbro…

MARY. And Papa
Is our time's finer craftsman.

(Silence)

OLGA. I would like for you
To listen to this Vivaldi piece,
My darling. Let's go inside.

CHAPTER FOUR

"May I, for my own self, song's truth reckon,
Journey's jargon, how I in harsh days
Hardship endured oft."
　　—"The Seafarer"

1.

The hospital was institutional, efficient and cold. The patients would check in and never check out again. They would roam the halls, smearing feces on the walls. They would roam the halls, muttering incomprehensible things about spies and bugs in their brains and microphones imbedded in their teeth and tiny computers stuck in their brains. They roamed the halls, dreaming of escape to a paradise island or walked the halls with their heads filled with phantasmagoria, slaves to their madness. They roam the halls. They are everywhere, muttering, mumbling, shuffling their feet, their eyes dead and vacate, almost as if they were zombies, which in a sense they were. They were experiments in living, living embodiments of how policy towards the mentally ill had not progressed much in the 20th century. They roam and will roam and will roam forever in these halls, until they expire and go to heaven. Why heaven? Because St. Elizabeths was already hell. So they roam the halls, stumbling along because of their medications; they stumble and mumble and grumble and slowly, slowly, they crumble.

There were routines that all the patients had to follow,

no matter how far off the planet they were. Regularly doctors came to interview them, and they would sit for an hour or two answering their inane queries. Pound was no exception. He would be interviewed like any other patient. He was insane, that was the given, so they generally took it from there. They did not expect cogent remarks; they did not want brilliance. If you played the game, they would play it too. That was the only way to survive. But early on Ezra did not know the game. He was still sincere about his answers. He framed everything by his masterwork, *The Cantos*. How did qualia fit into that super-structure? There were many layers to the poem, but also multiple surfaces, like a Cubist painting by Braque or Picasso. Wasn't it Pablo who once said to him that the meaning of life is to find your gift. Then he puffed on a Gitanes. The purpose of life, Picasso said, is to give it away. But Pound knew that Picasso gave nothing away; there was a price for everything. He was a cold, calculating, conniving genius, Pound thought, and so he liked him, not nearly as much as he liked Gaudier-Breska or any number of other painters and sculptures he had met in Paris. Besides, meaning did not interest poets; meaning was a low-grade mug's game in the scheme of things. Who cared what something meant? What mattered to Pound was the sound, the rhythms, what he called the rhythms of experience. What mattered was the concision, to be precise, the exact image. What did Eliot call it? Ah, yes. The objective correlative. A deep image, one that was freighted with emotions and feelings, associations and trembling certainty. Ezra was sat there in his baggy trousers and plimsolls on his feet, a bulky knit sweater that some admirer had given him to wear because he had complained of the drafts in the bug house. He wore a bright colorful scarf, the hangman's knot, the way the British wore their scarfs, but not the French, not the Spanish, not the Italians. At least the bloody British did one thing right, he thought.

Then he realized that the new doctor was talking to him.

The doctor said: Just a couple of preliminary points, Mr. Pound.

—Doctor Pound.

The doctor ignored him.

—You are Criminal No. 76028. Is that correct?

Pound did not, would not, answer. He was silent.

—Mr. Pound?

—Doctor.

—Yes.

—Doctor Pound.

—And here at the hospital you are Case No. 58,102. It is important for you to remember this information. Now let's get down to business. Lovely day out there.

—Lovely, Pound said, flatly, and he stared out the window, not making eye contact with his new doctor. It is safe to say that no one at St. Elizabeths had ever seen the likes of Ezra Pound, and no one knew quite how to deal with him.

—Tell me about your childhood, the doctor said.

—My childhood?

—Yes.

—Fuck my childhood, Pound said, again flat and affectless.

—Were you happy?

—I was happy as Larry, EP said.

The doctor looked down his nose at his patient. The doctor balanced his glasses on the tip of his nose and he stared over his glasses at this patient. Case No. 58,102. He asked the patient whether Larry was his friend.

—Was he a friend?

Pound looked frustrated. But he kept his powder dry.

—It is an expression, doctor.

—Ah, the doctor said. An expression. Now we are getting somewhere. An expression of what, Ezra? And from where?

—From across the sea, Pound told him. Europe.

—Italy? the doctor asked.

—No, not Italy, Ezra said.

—Paris?

—If by Paris, you mean France…

—Where?

—London, Ezra said.

Without losing a beat, the doctor said: You seem obsessed with European things, Mr. Pound. Is that true?

—Doctor.

—Yes.

—I'm Doctor Pound.

The doctor would appear to be fed up with his patient's behavior.

—Do you have a medical degree? he asked Ezra Pound.

—I have a fucking doctorate of humanities.

The doctor ignored him.

—You mentioned London. What does London mean to you? Who is Larry and why are you as happy as Larry? Is he your comparator?

—It means nothing, said Ezra, giving up on making a connection with this young doctor.

—Why?

—Why?

—Yes.

Pound laughed.

—We are going down a rabbit hole, doctor.

—Meaning?

2.

EP. I am disinclined to follow a line
Of discourse such as this. I am tired.
Don't you understand.
I'm exhausted, by the noise here,
By the lack of privacy, by doctors
And nurses and orderlies
Poking and probing me
All hours of night and day.

DOCTOR. What about your childhood?

EP. What about it?

DOCTOR. Did you have a happy childhood
Like your friend Larry did?

EP. This is another rabbit hole.

DOCTOR. Because of childhood trauma?

EP. Because I have been poked and probed
For months and months and months;
Because I have been demeaned;
Because I have been misunderstood.
I am not treasonous. I am the opposite
Of being a traitor. I am a patriot.
I am like Adams and Jefferson.
I believe in the Constitution, though
I may be an originalist, I may think
We need to return to the original values
That were laid out in that founding document.

The doctor asked if Pound felt persecuted because of his
ideas and his beliefs.

Pound had had enough of this line of questioning.

—You are a fucking idiot, he said.

—You seem very aggressive today. Would you like more
medication.

EP. They had me in a cage for months
In Pisa. They had me in a gorilla cage.
And where are my Confucian notes?
Someone misplaced them at the jail
When we landed here in bloody Washington.
They had me outside in a cage for months,
In the elements, amid the dust and rain,
My fellow prisoners being executed,
One by one. I am six feet tall,
And the cage was six feet high.
I walked bent over. I'll never straighten out
Again. It has ruined my spine, my posture.

DOCTOR. This was in Italy?

EP. Yes, in Pisa.

DOCTOR. And Pisa is Italy?

EP. You Americans know nothing
About geography, about
  The rest of the world.

DOCTOR. I believe that you are an American too.

EP. Yes, I am one of youse.
But I made a point
Not to become
A provincial.

DOCTOR. You think that other Americans
Are provincial compared to yourself.

EP. Pisa is in Italy.

The doctor sat looking at his notes. He finally said. You
haven't answered my question,

Ezra.

EP. I will put up with a certain amount
Of idiocy and ignorance, even
A certain amount of inconvenience.
But you fellows have been poking
And prying and probing and asking

Questions day and night, day after bloody
Fucking day. Mentally and physically,
I am tired. I am exhausted. I am an old man.
Enough is enough. *Basta cosi!*

"May I for my own self song's truth reckon,
Journey's jargon, how I in harsh days
Hardship endured oft.
Bitter breast-cares have I abided,
Known on my keel many a care's hold,
And dire sea-surge, and there I oft spent
Narrow nightwatch nigh the ship's head
While she tossed close to cliffs."

The doctor wanted to know if that was a poem that Ezra
liked. He asked the poet if he knew who wrote it. Is it from
childhood?
Pound smiled.
—No more childhood reminiscences.
—Because of trauma?
—Because I am bored.
Pound declared:
Bring me some books to read.
Give me a pen and paper to write with.
Even in Pisa, they let me have
Pen and paper and treated me with respect,
Called me Dr. Pound, gave me sheets,
Endless reams of paper to write my poems.
They let me use a typewriter
In the after hours, when the soldiers
Went off their shifts, and dreamed of home.

DOCTOR. What else?

EP. I'm claustrophobic. I need space.
I need exercise, a walk somewhere.
Even the Detention Center was better than this.
Even the DC prison was better than this.
Listen to the Bedlam all around us,
People screaming, smearing the walls
With their excrement. I thought at this age,
I would have written of Hell and Purgatory
By now, and I would be writing
My paradiso. Instead, I am prisoner
No. 76028. I am Case No. 58,102.
Do I look dangerous to you, doctor?

DOCTOR. No.

EP. I am not.
I am a poet.
I believe in my ideas.
The rhythms of action
And experience.
The direct treatment
Of the object.
Of *le mot juste*.
I was dear friends
With two of the
Greatest geniuses
Of our time,
T. S. Eliot and
James Joyce.

3.

But the doctor was ultimately not impressed by Ezra Pound. The doctor wrote down things in his notebook, observations of the patient. He asked Pound if he ever thought that maybe sometimes he was just a bit delusional. Pound pleaded with the doctor then:

—Doctor, doctor, I am Doctor Pound. Just like you. We are both doctors. I believe in *le mot juste.* Do you even know what that is?

—I'm afraid I don't, Mr. Pound.

—It's Flaubert, Ezra told him.

—Who?

—A writer.

—Another friend of yours? the doctor said sarcastically.

—Author of *Madame Bovary.*

Then the doctor took a different approach.

—Should I read it?

Pound brightened.

—Immediately, he said. There is no life to speak of without reading Flaubert. He once said: "*Madame Bovary, c'est moi!*"

—Meaning?

—Meaning that I need more room. I need to roam free.

—Do you know where you are? the doctor asked sternly.

—Every minute, Pound said. Every day.

—In lieu of prison and a death sentence, you have been sent here, to St. Elizabeths Hospital. We are just on the edge of the capital, Washington, DC. It is the autumn. You have been here for several months. You are not going to get out.

—Ever? Pound asked.

—Ever, said the doctor.

The doctor let that sink in.

—Let's talk about childhood. What were your parents like?

Pound was confused.

Who wouldn't be?

—What is there to say about one's own parents? They were lovely. I loved them. Still do. They gave me my life. They encouraged me wildly in everything I ever did. They were my biggest supporters, financially, emotionally, in every sense. They read my poems. They bought my books. They talked about me to their friends. I loved mom and dad.

—What were they really like? the doctor asked.

EP. I want to hear the birds outside.
The birds are singing out the window.
Are they coming or going and which
Tree is that has most satisfied their birdness?
What did they stop for? Was it to say
Hello to me, their friend?
Da boids! Da boids!

DOCTOR. What does it mean,
These birds, what does it
Mean to you, hearing the birds?

EP. Look, doc, obviously I am not violent.
I don't shit on the floor. When do you plan
To get me out of this ward and into

Some place a little bit nicer than here?

DOCTOR. I'll see what I can do, Ezra.

(Doctor stands to leave)

EP. Oh, and another thing.

DOCTOR. Yes.

EP. I call you doctor,
And you call me Ezra.
I'm sixty years old.
You are probably
Not even forty yet.

DOCTOR. I'm forty-eight.

EP. Like you, I am a doctor.
If I have to call you doctor,
Why is it that you call me Ezra?

DOCTOR. I'll see you tomorrow,
Doctor Pound.

EP. Okay, Jerry, see you tomorrow.
Mañana. Abiento.

(Doctor exits the cell)

CHAPTER FIVE

"And your father, who was brave as a leopard,
Was governor in Hei Shu, and put down the barbarian rabble,
And one May he had you send for me,
　despite the long distance.
And what with broken wheels and so on, I won't say it wasn't
　hard going,
Over road twisted like sheep's guts."
　　　—"Exile's Letter"

**At the edges of this scene are the various inmates,
enacting their pantomimes.**

1.

They sit in Adirondack chairs on the lawn outside the building where Ezra is housed. It is the springtime, the sun shining, the birds in the trees, the leaves on the trees, the trees and the flowers in bloom. They sit on a flagstone patio in their Adirondack chairs. If you did not know it was an insane asylum, you might guess it was an exclusive country club for an eccentric assortment of people from around the world. As if making a political and an artistic statement, amid the chairs was a claw-footed old-fashioned white-porcelain bathtub. On its side was written these words: MAKE IT NEW. Ezra sits naked in the bathtub, indifferent to the oddness of his nakedness. He is in his late sixties, and some people think he has dementia; others think that he is a great conman, conniving and shucking and jiving everyone. His wife Dorothy sits in her Adironack chair in stark contrast to her husband, with his wild mop of gray hair and his birdsnest of a beard gracing the lower portion of his face, his eyes wild and intense like a falcon's or a red-tailed hawk. Dorothy is dour, dressed in muted grays and blacks, her sensible shoes on her feet, her hat a proper English one, tweedy and someone out of season. A very tall young poet sits beside Ezra and his wife Dorothy. Along with him, there is sat Spencer Albertson, a neo-Nazi and KKK member, wearing a Nazi shirt and storm-trooper boots. Thomas Jefferson is there, too, wearing traditional American 18th century kit, sat in a chair on the other side of Dorothy and Ezra; he wears a powdered wig and carries a tri-corn hat in his hands, and tiring of the conversation, gets up and walks around the gardens, taking in the man-made scene. Jefferson, dressed in his Colonial American kit, the shoes of another time, the stockings and the breaks, the waist-coat and the overjacket, with its swallowlike tails, and not to mention his tricorn hat and the powdered wig, looks a bit out of sorts. He is not quite fitting in with the others, including Ezra Pound, who conjured him in the first place. If it weren't for Ezra Pound, you could not even imagine Thomas Jefferson in such a bizarre setting.

At the edge of this bucolic scene, there are voluminous inmates, wearing inmate gear, shuffling and mumbling, al-most like a Greek chorus in a very weird rendition of a play by Aristophanes or perhaps it is a play by Euripides that has gone terribly wrong. No, no, it is more modern than that. This is a Brechtian scene, this bughouse aria, the crazy people the only sane ones, while the sane ones, whoever they might be, live beyond these lamps, beyond this pale, in their suburban worlds from Foggy Bottom. These commuters and faceless bureaucrats are the antithesis of Mr. Pound, Mr. Jefferson, and all these others.

2.

Charles Olson, the young poet, was a giant of a man. Six feet eight inches tall. He towered over everyone and everything. Ezra did not know what to make of him. On the one hand, Olson understood Ez's poetry as well as anyone, maybe even more so than anyone. But on the other hand, he was a Democrat; he'd even worked in the Roosevelt—that traitor—administration. He was a liberal, something Ezra found reprehensible. But sometimes Ezra couldn't complain too much about his visitors because he was lonely and needed company, and more than company, he needed an audience so that he might carry on his dream of the Ezuversity, lecturing to the chosen few who came to sit at his feet. Ez liked Olson on one level, and thought him a rube on another. But how could he have worked in that goddamn Roosevelt administration? That was something which Ezra could not fathom. But there was no denying that Olson knew Ezra's poetry. There was a handful of these young poets who did: Paul Blackburn, John Berryman, Robert Lowell. Olson could quote it chapter and verse, and he seemed to understand Ez's poetic intentions, the drift of the poem, and he was from New England. He spoke with a Gloucester accent, though he was from some place more inland than Gloucester. Ezra knew Gloucester from Eliot. Old Possum often talked about the North Shore of Boston. It was in his poetry, but it was also in his conversations. The Gloucesterman had read Pound some of his poetry; Ezra could see where he was coming from and what he was up to and he was flattered that Olson referenced him in the poetry and some of the cadences, the rhythms, seemed to be derived from *The Cantos*, so all in all, Olson was all right, and yet being who he was, Pound preferred the nutty characters with their weird conspiracy theories.

Spencer Albertson was just such a man, a neo-Nazi and a KKK member, he was seated in one of the Adirondack lawn chairs next to Charles Olson. Spencer had shown up wearing a sportcoat, but once on the inside of the compound, he took off his jacket and Ezra saw that he was wearing a Nazi Stormtrooper outfit. Lovely, Ez thought, a man after my own heart. A comrade in arms. Besides Charles Olson and Spencer Albertson, Dorothy sat in an Adirondack chair nearby, and next to her, standing, was Thomas Jefferson, which Ezra took to be auspicious. Jefferson had not visited St. Elizabeths Hospital previously. His wig was powdered and his colonial outfit was impeccable. Ezra smiled at Dorothy, nodding towards Jefferson, as if to say thank you to her for bringing him, either the real deal or a facsimile thereof; it did not matter, but only added to the dynamic of conversation, and one could not live life without some lively conversation. James Joyce knew it, and he'd taught Ezra Pound to listen when people spoke, that all the poetry he would ever need could be found there.

3.

—Olson, do you know Spencer?

Olson deadpanned his response.

—We've not had the pleasure.

On the spur of the moment, Ezra stood naked before the Neo-Nazi and Charles Olson. Buck naked, Ezra stepped out of the waterless tub, smiling wisely. He placed his clothing, neatly folded, on the back of an Adirondack chair. Then he climbed back into the gigantic porcelain tub.

Ezra looked at Olson and pointed towards Spencer.

—He's a fine fellow, Ezra said.

Olson had his doubts that Spencer Albertson was a fine fellow. He seemed to be nothing of the sort. The giant of a poet did all he could to restrain himself from standing and throttling Spencer with his gigantic hands. Instead Olson said:

—I am sure.

Dorothy piped up from the perimeter.

—Has your Jewish doctor spoken to you, Ezra?

Albertson looked astonished. He said to Mrs. Pound:

—Mr. Pound refuses to speak to any Jewish doctors.

Olson could no longer restrain himself. He said:

—That will exclude a lot of competent hands.

Spencer looked down his nose at Olson.

—Are you Jewish?

—Is the Pope a Catholic?

—What does that mean?

—You figure it out.

Pound came to Olson's defense.

—Charles is a Melville scholar.

—I'm also a poet.

Pound laughed. His laugh was strange and other worldly. Maniacal. Ancient, like a pyramid. Pitched in a way to suggest that laughter was not a familiar device in the Pound repertoire.

4.

EP. He thinks he's a poet.
But what is a poet?
Do poets bleed?
Do poets have feelings?
Is a poet a man?

OLSON. I know quite a few good woman poets, Mr. Pound.

EP. Call me, Ezra. We are all part of the Ezuversity,
Even yourself,
Mr. Olson.

SPENCER. Pound is my mentor.

EP. I've got Spencer reading Mussolini and Jefferson.

5.

Thomas Jefferson stepped up. He was tall and striking looking, dressed in his 18th century American pioneer clothing, but with a touch of Europe about him, probably from his stint in Paris. He had a Southern accent, one of those slow, slurry Virginia kinds, full of bourbonated opinion, though in Jefferson's case, he was not known as a profligate with the booze. He was a gentleman. And a scholar. He owned slaves, true, and was in love with one of them, and fathered many children with Sally. But, but, but...

—I am not a KKK bigot, Jefferson announced to the committee in front of him.

Pound looked at him quizzically, and so did Dorothy, while Olson and the Neo-Nazi Spencer Albertson did not seem to notice Jefferson at all, which is saying something, since he looked so majestic in his kit of Virginia gentleman.

—No one said you were, Pound said to Jefferson.

Olson looked around, wondering to whom Pound was speaking.

—I don't need Spencer Albertson reading my work.

Pound laughed good-naturedly.

—But are you really Thomas Jefferson?

Jefferson was amazed.

—Who else do you think I am?

Pound was honest.

—I thought maybe you were an hallucination.

—Maybe I am an hallucination. But that doesn't make me any less Thomas Jefferson.

Pound cleared his throat.

—I want to speak with you about my economic theories.

JEFFERSON. I'd rather speak to you
About the human voice,
    Its register,
And how it becomes
Spoken,
    And what that means
    To American poetry, sir.

Pound looked over at Charles Olson, the giant.

—Olson, Pound said, is this really Jefferson present and accounted for?

Charles wasn't sure if Pound was putting him on or if his mentor was really experiencing auditory and visual hallucinations. Anything was possible, given the circumstances. Take a sensitive person, a poet, put him in a cage for many months. Threaten him with death at a trial for treason. Lock him up forever in an insane asylum. What do you expect, that Mr. Pound is going to wake up with a clear conscience and his consciousness is such that he is finally at peace with his life and surroundings, his epic poem complete, his toys all in order? Give me a fucking break! Olson explained to the older poet that he (Olson) was there with Mrs. Pound and Mr. Albertson, the Neo-Nazi. Calling him that, Albertson took umbrage with Olson's description.

—I am not a Neo-Nazi, Albertson said. I'm a full-fledged Nazi, but of the American variety.

Pound was concerned with other matters. Olson could

see the worry in his face. Maybe Pound was on medications. There was a kind of human fog about the poet, as if he were some place entirely from where he was, which was an insane asylum on the edge of Washington, D.C. There was a slight tremor in the poet's voice.

—None of you see Jefferson?

Pound looked from face to face, searching for confirmation.

Finally Dorothy spoke up.

—He's here all right.

—How do you know?

Dorothy spoke with great certainty.

—I just heard him talking to you.

Pound smiled for the first time in forever. He looked at ease. He pat Dorothy's hand affectionately.

—You're all right, Dorothy, and I'm sorry for being harsh with you yesterday.

Dorothy saw her advantage and took it.

6.

—And the day before, and the day before that, and last week, you are always harsh with me.

—That is because you control everything about me now. It is not fair that I have no say.

Pound's voice sounded pleading and almost childish, pouty and irritated.

Dorothy was the grown-up in the room

—I always convey your wishes to the staff. How do you think I was able to secure this bathtub for you?

He had already dismissed her.

He said:

—I thought Confucius sent it.

Ezra nodded to the giant poet in their midst.

—Olson, read for me what the bathtub says.

Charles reluctantly obliged his mentor.

—MAKE IT NEW.

The older poet had an expansive grin on his face.

—Make it new, he said. Is that what you are doing with your poems and your prose?

Olson was sincere and earnest, two qualities that Pound didn't seem to appreciate in any way.

—Yes, Charles said.

—Day by day?

But in another sense Olson was unflappable.

—That is why I visit you, he said.

Ezra looked around conspiratorially, then staged whispered:

—You are not a government spy?

Olson was straight-faced and factual.

—No, he said. I am a fellow poet, a young poet, but I am greatly influenced by yourself and your good friend, William Carlos Williams.

Again, Pound looked around conspiratorially.

—There is no hidden agenda?

Olson was a bit frustrated. He answered:

—You ask me that question each time I visit you. But,

no, there is no hidden agenda, no secret cabal that I am employing to get you to confess to misdeeds.

Ezra was not wholly convinced about Charles, though.

—But you worked for Roosevelt?

Olson once again was there to straighten out the record.

—I worked for an undersecretary in the Office of the War, along with several other poets and writers.

Ezra wanted to know if Charles was not a missionary and he explained that he was not terribly fond of missionaries. He did not care for Christian belief systems, though he confessed to love the art of the Renaissance, but then who could not love Giotto or Fra Lippi Lippo? Charles explained that his own love was poetry, and secondarily he had an active interest in archeology, particularly Mayan ruins. Olson said that he had especially loved Pound's poetry. Dorothy seconded this opinion, saying, He loves your poetry, Ezra.

—And he's not a Jew?

Dorothy was confused.

—Not as far as I know, she answered, still nonplussed.

Spencer Albertson, the Neo-Nazi friend of the Pounds, put in his own two cents.

—Mr. Pound still finds Jews problematic, sir.

Charles looked at Spencer contemptuously. If a look could kill, Spencer had just been executed by Charles Olson.

—Shut up, you little shit, Olson said, under his breath and full of venom towards Spencer Albertson.

—What? the Neo-Nazi asked, not sure of where he stood

with Olson, though finally he was getting a hint.

—You heard me, Olson said.

Charles, being so large, was not easily provoked into a violent reaction. But Spencer had rubbed him the wrong way all afternoon. Finally, he was not able to take it any longer; he didn't want to go off on the Pounds, but Spencer Albertson was a far easier target, with little consequences for his spite.

Spencer looked around uncomfortably for an ally.

Pound, drugged up on tranquilizers that all the patients were given, still had the clarity of mind to follow the action on the patio that afternoon. To Dorothy he said:

—My money's on Olson, Dorothy. He has a longer jab. I predict a knockout in the first round.

But Olson was determined to relieve Pound of this notion about his (Charles') toughness in a fight.

—I am not a violent man, he said.

Pound laughed, patting Olson on the back.

—I didn't think you were.

Then they all fell silent and remained silent for a long time, the sound of birds and insects flitting about, the sound of the wind rippling in the leaves on the trees, or the sounds of the inmates, shuffling about, were the only sounds that seemed to envelop the afternoon and all the guests on the patio.

7.

Pound was thinking about poetry again. He mentioned some Chinese characters. Axe. Tree. To renovate. Olson said: Between them the son.

—Fascism, Pound said, then smiled devilishly.

—Now, Ezra, Dorothy quipped.

He was just taking the piss, he told her, just having some fun.

—Be nice, Dorothy said.

—Fuck being nice, Pound told her. Being nice is what got me into this mess.

To Olson, Dorothy Pound said:

—He's just teasing you, Charles.

—I'm taking the piss, nuncle.

Olson was sincere and yet somehow naïve about how to respond.

—Shall I get a guard? he asked. Does Mr. Pound need to go to the lavatory?

Dorothy told Olson that that would not be necessary.

—Mrs. Pound?

—Can't you see, she said. Nothing is real here. Not the shrubs. Not the scenery. It is all an illusion.

Olson pointed towards the bathtub that sat on the patio along with the lawn chairs. On the side of the old tub, with its claw-foot legs, was that inscription in big capital letters.

—And the tub? he asked.

—It's Ezra's metaphor. He sits in his own metaphor. It isn't real. He made it up. It's an illusion.

—And St. Elizabeths?

—Total illusion, she said.

Pound laughed.

Dorothy explained to the young poet what she meant.

—You see a great poet. Good. It is good to see that in another person.

Dorothy sipped her tea and put down the cup on a small table beside her chair.

—But I see a broken old man, she cried out.

Olson looked confused.

—Which one is it? he asked.

—You tell me, Mr. Olson, Dorothy said, looking most proper and upright, weary and yet somehow still striking in her dress and how she carried herself and how life had thrown this curveball their way late in the game.

—You tell me, Dorothy said.

Chapter Six

"and there was a smell of mint under the tent flaps
especially after the rain'
and a white ox on the road toward Pisa
as if facing the tower,
dark sheep in the drill field and on wet days were clouds
in the mountain as if under the guard roosts."
—"Canto LXXIV"

St. Elizabeths Hospital. A common room, decorated
with crepe for Halloween.
Present are many patients,
all dressed in various costumes
reflective of Ezra Pound's life and poetry.
For instance,
there is Thomas Jefferson, Confucius,
Dante & Cavalcanti, John Adams, James Joyce,
T.S. Eliot, Mussolini,
Holocaust survivors in striped pajamas, etc.
Patients scurry about in their costumes,
Doing the Thorazine shuffle.

1.

EP. Where is my fool,
My Caliban,
My monster?

LEROY. Here I is, boss.

EP. Where were you, sirrah?

LEROY. Shakin' the snake,
Takin' a piss,
Having sex
With the nurses.

EP. You devil.

LEROY. I am not a traitor.

EP. Then how did you
Wind up
In the Bughouse
With all us
White devils
And crazies?

LEROY. I fucked your mother, Ezbo.

EP. Leave my mother
Out of it,
Monster.
Anyhow,
   She's back
In Rapallo.

LEROY. Then it was your sister
I shtooped.

EP. I'm an only child.

LEROY. You act like an only child.
You stink of privilege, even
At this extremity
Known as the Bughouse, fool.

EP. I am King Ezra tonight.

LEROY. Your real name is fool,
'cause every other name you had
You lost
When you signed yourself into
The Bughouse.

EP. I resemble that.

LEROY. An educated man who had everything.
Good family. An intelligent, worldly man.
Traveled. Experienced in the world.
Important friends,
Awards and honors,
Books, good health,
And none of it was good enough
To keep you away
From becoming
A permanent resident of the Bughouse.
How you 'splain that, King Ez?
All I knows is that I was fucking
Someone in that linen closet
When you so rudely interrupted me
With your foolish plans
For Halloween.

EP. Maybe you fucked yourself.

LEROY. Maybe I did.
Maybe I was.
You certainly fucked yourself.
How else you 'splain
An educated white man
A jew-hatin'
Race baitin'
Honky from the high end
Philadelphia
A white-shoe ofay
Dr. Ezra Pound,
   How else you 'splain
Him among us
In these Bughouse blues,
Singer
Spiritualist &
Mentor
To this poor uneducated
Black soul
Who was found guilty
Of to be insane
      By reason of being Black.

EP. Don't give me
The magilla, Caliban,
Give me it
      Concise

With *dichtung*,
I want the deep image
Of why

And when
& how
You are here,
Boy.

LEROY. Guilty of being black
Whilst walkin' down
The streets

In broad daylight
    Of the nation's capitol.

EP. In the good old days,
They'd lynch
Your sorry black ass, fool.

LEROY. Today,
They threw me in the Bughouse
Singing
 The blues
With Dr. Pound.

EP. The doctor is in,
Monster.

LEROY. The doctor ain't in,
Ezrow,
The Doctor,
He be way out,

He's a traitor
To his education,
To his beliefs,
His friends

& his country.

They gonna lynch your smart ass, Ezbo

Once they find out
That you ain't really crazy.

Youse as smart as
A fox
Or the head of a wolf pack.
You as tricky
As a murder of crows.

You one tricky dude, Ez Pound.
You as smart as
  The man himself.

EP. Dr. Overholster?

LEROY. Dr. Holster,
He gonna shoot you 'tween the eyes,
Once he realize that he's been had,

& the ayes have it,
The nayes be damned.

EP. You are like my long lost son, Leroy.
As my friend
Wild Bill Williams
(a real doctor)
Says

You gots the Murkan idiom
Flowing
Through your beastly soul.

LEROY. I got rhythm.

EP. Who could ask for
Anything
More?

2.

They entered the common room in ones and twos and
sometimes threes and fours and even occasionally in a
group of five inmates. They were on parade; after all, it was
Halloween. They had worked hard on their costumes. Ezra
had helped them; he was the one who had gotten some to
dress like John Adams and Thomas Jefferson. He was the
one who got some of them to dress like James Joyce and T.
S. Eliot. Some of them walked around and around in circles
and others stared out the windows and some others still
shuffled like zombies, which some of them were, wearing
costumes and, some, in their Bughouse uniforms, gray and
somber and dour and stinking of loneliness and stinking of
institutional neglect, of years and years of being shuttled off
the coil of commerce, the coil of reason, into these despa-
rate straits. Ah, but Halloween was a great event, even in
the Bughouse.

Ezra Pound wore a cape and a slouch hat and a flamboy-
antly long knitted scarf with the same Chinese characters

that had been written on the bathtub out on the patio in front of the main building where they were now assembled inside.

One inmate wore an eye patch like James Joyce and had on tight-fitting European clothing, and even patent leather loafers, though where he had found this stuff, no one knew. Next to him stood a fellow dressed like T. S. Eliot in a pin-striped suit with a stiff, high white collar and with a tie, hair slicked back, backbone as straight as a rail. Other inmates were dressed like Dante Alighieri and Guido Cavalcanti, the Italian poets of the early Renaissance in Florence. There was Confucius, walking about in his ancient Chinese scholars outfit, saying hello and greeting everyone. Someone was even dressed like the poet H.D., Hilda Doolittle, Pound's college girlfriend at the University of Pennsylvania.

If Ezra hadn't instructed the inmates on what costume to wear, he would have imagined that the real H.D., the real Eliot or Joyce, were present in the common room.

Leroy and Ezra looked like the Fool and his Master, a bit like King Lear on the Heath, during the famous storm.

Music played, a string quartet made of in-house patients. Crazy people were often gifted people. You didn't go crazy if you weren't sensitive. Without being sensitive, you might as well be a corporate raider or a Supreme Court judge.

People ate cake, though some of the inmates smeared their cake on the walls. Some of the cakes were chocolate, some vanilla; some had lemon icing; others were carrot and zucchini cakes; oatmeal cookies. Everything had been freshly baked by the institution's cafeteria staff, all of whom loved coming to this event every year. But this was the first Halloween with Ezra Pound at the helm of the inmates.

Ezra had introduced a few new costumes and now some of the inmates were unfurling banners that they had worked on since the middle of summer.

One inmate's banner read:

SENESCO SED AMO / I GROW OLD BUT LOVE

Another banner read:

IL SESORO DI UNA NAZIONE E LA SUA HONESTA /
A NATION'S TREASURE IS ITS HONESTY
EQUITY IS THE TREASURE OF STATES

A third banner said:

COSI' VIVERE CHE I TUOI FIGLI E I LORO DISCEN-
DENTI
TI RINGRAZINO
SO LIVE THAT YOUR CHILDREN AND THEIR DE-
SCENDANTS
 WILL BE GRATEFUL TO YOU

The inmates marched around the room with the Fascist banners. The staff seemed ignorant of the references, though, so no one was in trouble quite yet. But if you looked over at Ezra Pound, a sly, sinister smile crossed his otherwise blank poet's face.

More and more banners were unfurled and marched around the common room at the hospital.

LUCRO PRIVATO NON CONSTITUTUISCE LA PROS-
PERITA
PRIVATE PROFIT DOES NOT CREATE PROSPERITY

L'ARCERE CHE MANCA IL CENTRO DEL BERSAGLIO
CERCE LA CAUSA DELL'ERRORE DENTRO SE STESSO
THE ARCHER WHO MISSES THE BULLSEYE SEEKS
THE SOURCE
OF THE ERROR WITHIN HIMSELF

LA PUREZZA FUNGE SENZA TERMINE, IN TEMPO
E IN SPAZIO
SENZA TERMINE
THE LIGHT OF HEAVEN ACTS WITHOUT LIMIT, IN
TIME AND IN SPACE
WITHOUT LIMIT

UN NAZIONE CHE NON VUOLE INDEBITARSI FA
RABBIA AGLI USURAI!
A NATION THAT WILL NOT GO INTO DEBT PUTS
THE USURER
IN A RAGE

THE POLITICAL HAS NOTHING IN COMMON WITH
THE MORAL

OUR RIGHT LIES IN FORCE

VIOLENCE MUST BE THE PRINCIPLE AND CUN-
NING, AND
CUNNING AND MAKE BELIEVE THE RULE)

3.

HD. Professor Pound of the Ezuversity?

EP. HD! Love of my early life! Imagist! Speak!

HD. I break a staff.
I break the tough branch.
I know—

I can't remember the rest.

EP. I know no light in the woods.

HD. I know no light in the woods.

EP. I have lost pace with the winds.

HD. I have lost pace...

EP. With the winds.

HD. With the winds.

EP. Excellent, my love.
You take me back to the U of P,
And my undergraduate days,

HD and I swanning about,
In love,
With each other,
And...

HD. With poetry.

EP. Yes, in love with poetry.
Excellent. Excellent.
I am the king of misrule.

LEROY. The fool and his fool.
Which one is which?
Try to guess.

4.

(James Joyce and William Butler Yeats, the latter wearing an ascot and a pince-nez)

JOYCE. Whiskey, whiskey,
My kingdom for a thimbleful,
A thumb's worth
A groat
The breath of life.

YEATS. You're drunk.

JOYCE. You should be drunk.

YEATS. It does not agree with me.
I don't even like strong tea.

JOYCE. If you want to commune
With spirits, Willy,
You need to have spirits
Within you.
        Whiskey is like the Holy Ghost.

It's there
    And not there.
A host.

YEATS. I am tired of Paris.
I need to go back to Coole Park
In Clare.

JOYCE. I don't care.
Go where you will.
Paris is my oyster.

EP. Stick to the script.

JOYCE. I thought you said I could improvise.

EP. Improvisation doesn't mean you haven't already
Mapped out the route that you wish to take.
It means that within a set of rehearsed improvisations,
You will create the illusion of spontaneity.

JOYCE. I'm fucking confused, Mr. Pound.

EP. Don't break character!

JOYCE. It's Irish, Ez.

EP. What's Irish?

JOYCE. Halloween. It's called Samhain.
It's Irish, pard.

EP. (Delightedly) Bullocks, Joyce.

JOYCE. Go on now, Ez.
You'd be taking the piss
With me once again.

EP. I thought you were dead.

JOYCE. I've been dying a death so long,
I'm dead that the dead in me story
Aptly called "The Dead."
But we all come back on Samhain.

EP. Do I owe you money?
You were always broke.

JOYCE. I owe you a debt of gratitude.
And it turns out that I was wrong
About this after-life.
It's teeming with circumstance.
Everyone's there.

EP. Who?

JOYCE. Dante.

EP. Who else?

JOYCE. He'll be by
Momentarily.

(Pause)

Who else?
Cavalcanti.

(Suddenly out of character)

Am I doing all right, Mr. Pound?

EP. Excellent, comrade.

JOYCE. Did I get the names right?

EP. It was as if James Joyce himself
Were present before us.

(Joyce goes off.
Dante & Cavalcanti step up.
They walk around, with Pound,
as if taking a stroll on the passeggiata,
arm in arm, talking)

5.

DANTE. *Guido, vorrei che tu e Lapo ed io*
Fossimo presi per incantamento,
E messi ad un vascel, ch'ad ogni vento
Per mare andasse a voler vostro e mio.

EP. Guido, I wish that you and Lapo and me
Were taken, as if by enchantment,
And placed on a boat, with every wind
Might sail the sea at your wish and mine.

DANTE. *Sicche fortuna, ed altro tempo rio,*
Non ci potesse dare impedimento,
Anzi, vivendo sempre in un talento,
Di stare insieme crescesse il disio.

EP. No storm or inclement weather
Could stop us,
But instead, living always in harmony,
Our wish to stay together would grow.

CAVALCANTI. *E monna Vanna e monna Lagia poi,*
Con quella ch'e sul numero del trenta,
Con noi ponesse il buon incantatore:

EP. And Ms. Vanna and Ms. Lagia then,
And the lovely number from number thirty,
A benign enchanter would put safely with us.

DANTE. *E quivi ragionar sempre d'amore:*
E ciascuna di lor fosse contenta,
Siccome io credo che sariamo noi.

EP. And there among us we would have reason
To talk perpetually of love, each one of us content,
Just as I believe that we would be.

(Pause)

Ah, bene, bene, molto gentile, amici.
Thank you, thank you, friends.

DANTE. *Prego, dottore, prego.*
Did I get it right, Poundy?

EP. Poundy, he like, molto.
Mi lo piace molto.

DANTE. *Va bene.*

EP. Now, Guido.
Cavalcanti, it's your aria.

CAVALCANTI. I can't remember
A fucking thing, Ez.

EP. What's the matter?

CAVALCANTI. It's the meds.
My memory is shot.
English is hard enough
To remember,
But Italian,
Forget about it.

EP. Try, try.
Forget about the Italian.
Do it in English.

CAVALCANTI. A lady asks—
I can't remember the rest, Ez.

EP. A lady asks me…

6.

(HD, Dorothy Pound, and Olga Rudge appear)

HD. He was always an egoist, ladies.

OLGA. He had his charms.

DOROTHY. Such as?

OLGA. He was a great lover.

DOROTHY. I don't want to hear about it,
Ms. Rudge.

LEROY. (Shouting) Let's keep to the racial
Stereotypes, if you please.
        It was I, me, Leroy,
That these ladies wanted to fuck,
And whom I did fuck,
Not Ezra Pound,
Who has not
Had a hard-on
Since he arrived here.
[Singing jazzily]

Salt Peter,
Salt Peter,
Salt Peter.

EP. Now let's leave the improv
To the players, monster,
And keep to our script.

LEROY. You ain't no Prospero, Pound.

EP. Ladies! *Encore une fois*!

HD. He took me to a Halloween ball
When we were courting
In college
    Back in Philadelphia.

EP. I'd rather be in Philadelphia.

LEROY. I'd rather be anywhere
But in this Bughouse
        Wid you lot.

DOROTHY. I don't wish
To share him
With anyone, thank you.

He's my husband, not yours or yours.
I'm his only wife.

OLGA. Get a life! He only loved me.

HD. He loved my poems.

(Pause)

EP. Stick to the script—
The goddamn script,
Sing goddamn, goddamn,
Goddamn, because I am.

Fellow loonies, stick
To what I wrote,
What we agreed
     To do.
Encore une fois!

DOROTHY. You're a controlling,
Manipulating weasel,
Ezra Loomis Pound.

EP. You should talk!
I am nothing
Of the kind.

All I asked:

Recite the words
On the page.

Is that too much
To ask?

OLGA. Where's the cake?

HD. I'd rather dance than recite.

7.

LEROY. Me, I prefer to fuck
Than do just about anything else.

They claim we wound up here
Because we couldn't fit in.

I'm here to tell you
That we're here because

We are not all there. I'm here—
We're here—because

We did try to fit in,
And look how terribly we failed.

EP. Failure is good.
To experiment,
To be human,
It is all to fail.

LEROY. Some of us fail grandly,
King Liar, but that would not be
You or me, Knucklehead.

We are a special kind of failure—
Human failures—
That wound up
In the Bughouse,
     Singing
The Bughouse
Blues.

ATTENDANTS. Medication!
Medication! Get your medication!
Step right up
And get your meds!
Everyone line up!

Chapter Seven

"Amo ergo sum, and in just that proportion"
— "Canto LXXX"

Sherry, young and beautiful and American, was there to entertain the poet. He called her his muse. They had been carrying on since she first appeared, going off into the bushes like a couple of teenagers while Dorothy Pound entertained the visiting dignitaries, young poets and publishers, academics who were sometimes just curious and occasionally were there to help Pound in any way they could. Dorothy dealt with them, while Ezra slipped off "into the woods" with Sherry. They fucked in the woods on the ground, their lovers' bed a pile of mulching leaves. It reminded Ezra of the Greeks, the ancient ones, and their priapic concerns in their goat songs and dithyrambic rites, the leather phalluses and Aristophanic jokes about dirty old men and beautiful young women, and the great thing for him was that Sherry was completely game. She was up for a roll in the leaves with the master, their age difference almost too great to calculate, but was probably forty years, and irrelevant. Naked, as she stood there in the woods, he remembered Picasso. He wondered what Picasso would think of Sherry. Picasso would love her breasts, he decided, and so would half of Paris and all of London, the British being obsessed with breasts, he decided, right there, on the spot. Look at their paintings; look at their Restoration costumes. Yes, Picasso was the one who might appreciate a naked Sherry. Ma Sherry, he thought, Ma Cherie, ma femme. Well, not his femme; Dorothy was that. Sherry was his muse, his inspiration, the object of his desire.

She ran from tree to tree, calling him, and he tripped after her, *il dottore, il professore.*

Back at the patio, Pound took off his clothes again, only this time in front of everyone, and sat in the bathtub. It was an illustration of *The Cantos*, specifically "Canto LIII," as it said on its side: MAKE IT NEW. *Tching had prayed on the mountain and wrote MAKE IT NEW on his bath tub, day by day make it new.* There Pound sat, as he said, a human being within his own metaphor.

—Only a poet could be so clever, he said.

The guests chuckled. No one there was unfamiliar with his shenanigans. Pound was nothing if not a great disrupter.

He invited Sherry to join him in the tub, and she did, only she did not want to take off her clothes in front of Dorothy and the other guests.

—He's so cute, she said, ruffling his messy long gray hair on top of his head.

—Is she real? Ezra asked his fans, this audience on the patio.

—Unfortunately, yes, Dorothy said, rather drolly.

—It's not an illusion, Pound said. But it is an allusion.

The poet Paul Blackburn was there that afternoon. He was small and thin with jet black hair and pale skin, wearing dark glasses and a big black cowboy hat. He took out a bottle of Fundador brandy and offered the bottle to the crowd, but there were no takers. Instead, he took a big slug himself.

—Ah, he said. That's good.

He took out a pack of Gitanes cigarettes and offered them around, but again there were no takers, so he took one for himself, lit it and inhaled.

The smell of the tobacco was strong and pleasant.

Charles Olson was also present, sitting next to Paul Blackburn, and he tried to engage Pound in some repartee or to get some wisdom from the master regarding the general craft of poetry. He said:

—What does not change / Is the will to change.

—Did I say that? Pound asked.

Olson explained:

—It is the opening line
Of my poem
"The Kingfishers."

EP. But I sd it.

SHERRY. You said it all, Ez.

OLSON. You did say it.

EP. It's my line.

OLSON. An allusion.

EP. But it's my line.
You got it from me.

OLSON. In a manner of speaking.

SHERRY. 'Splain to Ez.

(Pause)

OLSON. You got it elsewhere.

EP. Moi?

OLSON. Yes.

**(Sherry takes off her shoes,
And some of her clothes,
And steps into the tub
With Ezra Pound)**

Ezra explained that his muse, Sherry, distracted him. He could not keep his eyes off of her, nor his hands, he explained. His blood boiled. His heart fluttered, especially when Sherry bared them and asked the poet what he thought of her breasts. There is nothing about you, Sherry, he said, that isn't perfect. Dorothy Pound sat there no longer fuming; she had given up indignation long ago.

—There is nothing about you that isn't perfect, *ma cherie, ma Sherry*.

Then to Olson, EP asked:

—How tall are you, Olson?

Olson told him that he was six feet eight inches tall.

—Then you are a giant of a poet.

Charles was in a beneficent mood for the crotchety Pound and told the old man that he was every inch a poet. He went on to say that he could only approximate what it was that Pound had already accomplished.

—You are the giant of a poet, Olson said. I am only very tall.

When the various poets, young and old, came to visit, they became used to Pound's moods. He sometimes sat glumly in the Adirondack chair, staring off to the distant trees. At other times, he was exuberant about the smallest things in life, grateful for what he had, which after all was considerably more than any of the other inmates at St. Elizabeths Hospital. The criminally insane did not usually get afforded any luxuries in their lives, while Ezra Pound was given more liberties than any other patient. He had his own room; he even had a study lined with books. Granted, the study was in a hallway and not very private. But compared to the others, Pound was in paradise instead of the inferno. Pound's moods came on like the weather; sunny one minute, it was dark and ominous the next. The pleasure of Sherry had passed, and his priapic dream with her had passed along until another day. Somehow the idea of where he was, in an insane asylum, a world renowned poet, would creep up on Pound and bite him on the ass. The pain subsided and then a dull ache took hold; then he drifted back into a depressed state.

Such a gloomy state enveloped him in front of the assembled guests on the lawn in front of the main building where Pound lived. At the end of the day, everyone would leave him, including his wife Dorothy; they would go home to dinners at home in Washington, D.C., while he settled down to do his writing, the only thing that could distract him from his circumstances.

—All the rest is dross, he said to no one in particular.

But everyone present took it in.

All was dross.

Sherry was back in the bathtub, naked down to her underpants and called to her poet-lover:

—AMO ERGO SUM, Sherry said. I love therefore I am.

Dorothy ignored her.

To Olson, she said:

—He's like this every day.

Olson was alarmed.

—How do you stand it? he asked.

Dorothy said that he had been this way for as long as she had known him.

—All the rest is dross, Pound shouted. Then to Olson he asked: Who said that, Giant?

Charles was glad to be back in terrestrial communication with the old poet.

—You, he said, smiling.

Pound asked him who said that nothing changes / but the will to change.

Olson smiled.

—I did, sir.

—No, I did, Pound shouted.

—And Herbert Spencer, Olson said.

—Fuck Herbert Spencer, Pound called out.

—What did I do? Spencer Albertson asked.

—Not you, nuncle, Old Ez said. Herbert, Herbert.

—Oh, Spencer Albertson said.

—And who gives a damn about Herbert Spencer, Olson? He's a liberal jellyfish, a spoiled onion, just the way the streets of London smelled at night. Am I right, Dorothy?

Dorothy smiled the smile of the husband-weary wife.

—You are never wrong, dear, except when you are.

Pound seemed to be tone-deaf suddenly, as he didn't hear the sarcasm in Dorothy's voice.

—Except when I am, he said. *J'ayme donc je suis.*

That caught Pound's girlfriend Sherry's attention.

—I love therefore I am, she said, not to anyone present on the patio in front of the main building, but only to Ezra Pound himself, who caught her words upon the wind and seemed to deposit them in a safe in his heart.

—And, Olson, who else said that what does not change / is the will to change?

—Heraclitus, he said tentatively.

—But surely Heraclitus got it from me.

—No, no, Olson said seriously, lacking a sense of fun the way Pound had it.

—Joyce would say that I'm taking the piss, *il miglior' fabbro* said. That I'm taking the mick with you. Nobody could take the mick quite like Jimmy Joyce. I loved that man. He was consumed by the divine fire of genius, a Celtic genius.

To Olson, Dorothy Pound said: He was always fond of Jimmy Joyce.

—Fond is not the word. I was in the presence of genius. Just like I was in the presence of genius when I met Tom Eliot, Old Possum. There were others. Wyndham Lewis. Ford was a genius. *The Good Soldier.* That's a work of genius. Hemingway is a kind of genius with his shorter prose.

It was as if someone had just wound up Pound, because suddenly he had become animated once again.

—Gaudier-Brzeska was a sculptural genius. Picasso and Picabia, they were geniuses too. But no one possessed the divine, no one possessed the divine fire, no one had that divine fire of genius quite like James Joyce had it.

It was just then that a gentleman seemingly from another era seemed to wander into the patio area. He was dressed in what could only be called Revolutionary War kit, the tri-corn hat, the brigs, the buckled shoes, the waistcoat, the tails.

It was Thomas Jefferson.

—I seem to have lost my way, he said.

—Impostor! Pound shouted.

But no one present was sure to whom or what he referred. The people on the patio looked around but saw no one.

—Where's the medical staff when you need them? Pound asked. Then to the figment, Pound said:

—Did I ever tell you how Jimmy Joyce pronounced the word *book*? Say *boo.*

—Boo, Jefferson said.

—Now close it up by pronouncing the "k" at the end of it.

—Book!

—Excellent! Pound shouted.

To Olson, Spencer Albertson said:

—That "K" reminds me of the KKK.

—I need to go, Olson said.

Pound told Olson that he was too liberal, and that was his problem. He said that it was not Olson's poetry, not the words or even the music of those words. It was his politics that disturbed Ezra Pound.

—Olson, it's your damn liberal politics.

—I don't think so, he answered Pound. I'm post-liberal, even postmodern. I'm like the tansy flower.

—How are you like the tansy flower? Pound asked.

—I just am, Olson answered.

Pound looked deeply at him.

—You cannot be too smart for your own good, Olson.

Sherry wanted to know, from the horse's mouth (EP) what kind of spectre was he referring.

—Jefferson, Pound said.

—Apparently Thomas Jefferson has been visiting him in the afternoons lately. Go along with it.

Sherry was confused.

—Go along with it? she asked. If Ez thinks that Jefferson's here, who am I to contradict the master?

—Being too smart, Pound said, is an oxymoron. Except in my own case, in which case they locked me up and threw away the key. How long have I been here, Dorothy?

—Terribly long, she said in her most British way.

—I've been here terribly long, Jefferson, Pound called

out to the visage that no one saw but Pound himself.

Olson looked at his watch and stood to leave. It was later in the afternoon, and the sky was overcast.

—It's getting late, he said.

—Take our friend Bill Williams, Pound said. Dr. William Carlos Williams.

—A great poet, Olson observed. A great teacher. He is a great man.

Pound was not listening. In many respects, being at St. Elizabeths, he had lost his ability to listen the same way some old guy might lose his ability to hear, smell, taste, or see.

—Bill has always been confused, Pound told Olson. He is one of the reasons why I make so much about race. It is hard enough for a man to get this clear—this being this life, the world in which we find ourselves. It's hard enough when we are of one race.

—The white race, Spencer Albertson said.

—When a man is of one race, it's hard enough. But Bill Williams, he's French, Spanish, Anglo, and some wandering Jew from Saragossa—

—I have to go, Olson told Pound.

—You have let your mind be polluted by Roosevelt, Pound said, standing and jabbing his right index finger in the direction of Charles Olson. Franklin Finkelstein Roosevelt! Pound shouted. He is the war criminal, not the Duce, not even Hitler.

—Heil Hitler! Spencer Albertson stood and gave the Nazi salute upon the gloaming light on the patio in front of the main building of the insane asylum where Ezra Pound found himself gathered with this assortment of different people.

—You and Bill are polluted, he told Olson.

—I shall not be returning, Olson said.

Ezra Pound's frustrations exploded everywhere and nowhere at all. He seemed to be imploding from within, and he walked impatiently, anxiously, back and forth on the patio, his wild hair flopping everywhere, his loose clothes blowing in the wind.

He pointed at Olson, but no words came out, so he paced some more, then he stopped in his tracks.

—Do you want your Melville book back?

Olson waved his big hand.

—Keep it, he said.

Pound's voice was saturated with bitter sarcasm now.

—*Call Me Ishmael*, Pound said. Very clever. It is another labor-saving device.

Olson walked off without saying goodbye to anyone.

Dorothy now stood.

—I'm going back to my room, she told Pound.

Others seemed to gather around Dorothy and left with her, leaving only Sherry and the spectre of Thomas Jefferson.

—Me and the maestro, she said.

—And Jefferson, Pound told her. Let's not forget Tom. Are you prepared to discuss economics with me, Jeff?

JEFFERSON. I'm prepared to discuss
One thing and one thing only
With you, Ezra Pound.

There is really only one thing
That I have obsessed about
Throughout my whole life.

EP. The Constitution.

JEFFERSON. My love of Sally.

SPENCER. Sally?

JEFFERSON. Sally Hemings.
She was the love of my life.
I fathered several children
With her.
   She was my first wife's
Half-sister.

SPENCER. That's all right, sir.
We're all Southern gentlemen.

JEFFERSON. Sally Hemings
Was my slave. I freed all
Our children at the end
Of my life.
      But in this other life,
The one in which
I find myself now,

I can only think about her.

Her lips. Her voice.
Her breasts. Her tongue.

Her belly full with child,
Her belly empty.
Her legs, her arms,
Her blackness.

SPENCER. Her blackness?

SHERRY. This is exciting me,
Ezra.

EP. The Muse must be excited.

JEFFERSON. Economics?
I hardly ever think of it
Anymore. The Constitution?
It was written and it's done.
It was an imperfect perfection.
It was the thing itself.

But Sally, she was the love
Of my life,
        She was my real wife.
Only Sally was
  Perfect.

SHERRY. This is so cool.

EP. I am cold.
Where's a towel?
Where is my pen?
My notebook?
My typewriter?
Where did Olson go?

"yet say this to the Possum: a bang, not a whimper,
with a bang not with a whimper."
—"Canto LXXIV"

A tennis court at St. Elizabeths Hospital.
The late 1950s.
T. S. Eliot, dressed in formal tweeds,
holding a tennis racket.
EP wears light colored linen shirt and trousers,
tennis racket in hand.
There is no ball as they swat an imaginary one,
back and forth.

There he was: Thomas Stearns Eliot. He wore pinstripes. A stiff white collar, a proper British tie.

No one looked quite like Tom the Old Possum. His hair slicked back. His skin mortuary white. His eyes steely gray. His brogues shined into a dark lustre. He wore bright red socks, very foppish, Ezra thought, very English. Indeed. Tom was always a pleasure to see, whether it was London, Paris, or Rapallo. But circumstances prevented them for being in those former venues. Now they sat in the Adirondack chairs beside the run-down tennis courts. No one played tennis at St. Elizabeths except Ezra Pound. The two old friends sat with their chairs close to one another, their respective hearing having been compromised with age. If Eliot was another hallucination, it was a pleasant one, so that Ezra might think that, though he was tripping off the planet from time to time, the trips were becoming more enjoyable.

For instance, they played a game, Possum and Ez.

—No, said Eliot.

—Yes, said Pound.

—No, I say.

—I say, yeah.

—No, no; they would not.

—Yes, they have.

—By Jupiter, I swear, no.

—By Juno, I swear, ay.

They laughed uproariously.

It was great fun being in each other's company.

—That was good, said Eliot.

—Yes, said Pound.

—Now what?

They were silent.

Eliot stared off across the verdant lawns.

Pound went inward, scraping words from the side of his skull, something that might be socially acceptable, given his circumstances and all.

—Over there, Ezra said.

—Yes, Eliot answered

—There is a tree.

—Yes.

—A redbud.

—Oh, Eliot answered.

—This time of year, Pound said, not sure if what he was

saying was being understood.

—I see, Eliot said, suggesting that he did not understand the drift of the conversation.

—It blossoms, red as a baby's chafed arse.

—Ah, replied Eliot.

Then Tom paused. He said:

—In the beginning.

Now Pound was confused.

—The beginning? he said.

—Yes.

—What?

Eliot smiled.

—Is the end, he said.

—What?

Eliot smiled contentedly.

—It's a poem.

—Whose? Pound asked.

—Mine, said Eliot.

—Yours?

—Yes.

(Pause)

—What are we to do? Possum asked.

—About what?

Eliot did not like when others got emotional, but he especially did not like it when he could not control his own emotions, and seeing his old friend Ezra was putting his knickers in a twist. He stammered:

—About, about, you, sir.

Pound had been incarcerated at the hospital for years at that point.

There was a certain amount of acceptance of his circumstances. How else could he survive it, day after day, not of making it new, but simply surviving in this maelstrom of human misery.

—I'm all right, he lied. Then he was more truthful. He said:

—I've made my peace.

They were sat in Pound's "study," a part of a common area filled with bookshelves, books and his papers. But not really a private place, not really an "office" per se. You could hear the sounds of the other inmates, screaming and yelling at times, or just scraping along the walls, looking paranoid and lost. Women walked around mumbling to themselves; men might take a few steps, stop, shout aloud about birds or worms or people in their brains, then shuffle off their human coils, all sense of decorum abandoned.

The noise was the worst thing, how the voices echoed down the halls and how Pound's office was not in any out of the way place, but pretty much within the purview of the human traffic moving slowly, because of medication, up and down the halls.

Besides the unnerving sounds, there were the visuals, the patients truly gone, none of them on the cusp of sanity, waiting to be safe and taken home.

St. Elizabeths was a permanent solution even to temporary problems. Like a roach motel, you entered through its portals, but that did not mean you exited ever.

Pound quoted from the Irish, James Joyce specifically. He said:

—You only leave here one way, and that's feet first.

That means on a gurney, a sheet over your head.

Dead as a doornail.

But Pound he reconciled these contradictions about the sanitarium years earlier.

Eliot had been to the hospital before; this was not his first time to visit. But each time he came, which was not that often, he seemed to get himself unraveled the longer he stayed, the sounds and the images reminding, maybe, of his first wife Vivian, who also wound up in a similar accommodation as Eliot's friend Ezra Pound.

Ezra still had his rude health, whereas Tom looked more fragile, more human. Pound still strutted about as if he were an immortal or a demigod, his hair long and scraggly, his dress distinctly bohemian, the clothing baggy and flowing. He often walked about with his button shirt unbuttoned, his hairy powerful chest showing, even though it was full of gray hair.

Eliot was buttoned up and proper.

Pound was loud and rude, opinionated and stubborn, a force of resistance, even within the restrictions of St. Elizabeths. He had managed to get the heads of the place to see his point of view, which explains how he was given a typewriter, the books, the bookshelves, the desk, the chairs, none of which any other inmate had.

Most of his visitors were literary personages such as Mr. Eliot. But Pound still drew his fair share of nutters: Neo-Nazis, Fascists (Italian and American), Nazis, fringe believers, conspiracy theorists, bigots, and bullies of the Constitution, states righters, right-wing radio personalites, and wack-jobs of one sort of another, which Pound seemed to relish almost as much as he enjoyed the parries and thrusts with the literary lights.

—But the situation, Tom said.

—The Bughouse?

Pound looked around, taking in everything, and gestured grandly, as if he were the prince in his realm.

—St. Elizabeths, Eliot declared.

—Yes.

Eliot seemed lost for words.

—It's intolerable, he finally said. It's appalling, Ezra.

Pound disagreed.

After all, he was the patient. Eliot would go home afterwards or back to where he was staying, while Ezra had to line up for meals or visits to the shrinks which was a regular occurrence in such a facility. He would have to endure their poking and prodding into his personal life, the furthest reaches of his mind, not to mention every nook and cranny of his actual person, including the most private orifices of the body. Like a prison, the strip search was as regular as prayer might be in a monastery.

—No, it is not intolerable, because I do tolerate it. I don't just endure it, I prevail and I survive.

—You are a fighter.

Ezra smiled when Tom, Old Possum, said that.

—Remember the old days? he asked his old friend.

Eliot told Ez that no one could forget those days in London and Paris, but especially in London.

—Who could forget them, Eliot said, and then more philosophically, that is, until we actually forget them, because everything, sooner or later, is forgotten, including you and me.

—I edited you, Ezra declared proudly, as if being an editor would exempt him from the ravages of old age or time itself and its long arc, not into justice, but oblivion.

—And I edited you, Eliot assured him, even though you were not always open to my suggestions.

—Never!

—In a manner of speaking.

EP. In a manner of nothing-
Of-the-sort. I edited you.
You never edited me.
You needed editing.
You were prolix.
That is not a good quality
In a poet.

ELIOT. The poet may be
Whatever he wishes.
It is the poem
That cannot afford
To be encumbered by
Prolixity. But I did manage
To publish the Quartets,
Four Quartets
Without your editing.

EP. It shows.

ELIOT. Really?

EP. I'm taking the mick
With you.

ELIOT. That word, mick,
And that phrase, taking it,
It reminds me in its way
Of our old friend,
Mr. Joyce,
Dead these many years.

EP. I hardly think of anyone
From the past
Anymore,
    Unless it is the distant past,
In which case
        I think of Cavalcanti,
Pere Vidal,
    Dante...

ELIOT. Ah, Dante.

EP. Yes.

ELIOT. There was no one,
There is no one,
Quite...

EP. Yes.

(Silence)

Pound spoke to Eliot about the years, and how they go by. The years go by. Yes, Eliot agreed. Tempus fugit. Now they were old men, whereas once they were young ones. They were full of energy and ideas and their idealism about literature, as if words and their rhythms were everything; as if breath and syllable would solve all the problems of the known world, give it an order that it never had otherwise; give it direction and purpose, for without literature, it was as though everything were formless and going nowhere. Where did time go? The snows of yesteryear, Eliot laughed. Pound's old friend spoke about time past and time present, and then time future. But all Pound could ask was whether any of it *cohered*. Cohering seemed to be everything to Pound in those incarcerated days. Eliot asked him what he meant by his remark of cohering. What coheres? he asked Pound. Ezra seemed annoyed, if not with Eliot, whom he loved, then with life itself, which often confused Pound, especially given where he had ended up. Life had become a kind of Inferno that Ezra had been sentenced to, and yet he could not remember what the crime was.

—What coheres? he asked. Why, our lives, Possum. Our work, our writings.

—I have done what I could do, Eliot said. And soon I will be done.

Pound smiled broadly.

—But not John Donne.

Eliot demurely answered, as if Ezra were not a child but

a grown man full of responsibilities and purpose, which even Eliot could see that his old friend was not.

—No, not John Donne, he said. But I am here.

—Where?

—Here.

—But where is here? Venice. London. Paris.

—St. Elizabeths, Eliot said.

He waved his hand around the scenery, noting a particular tree, a plain tree, they called it in England. But here they called it a sycamore. At least this sycamore looks like a plain tree to Tom Eliot.

—I am visiting my old friend, Eliot said. My dear old friend.

—Me?

—Yes, you, Eliot told him. I am here visiting you.

Pound said that he considered it an honor. There had been many visitors over the years to the Bughouse, he said. But there were none more illustrious than his old friend, T. S. Eliot. Old Possum. When Ezra asked why Tom was there, Eliot said that he had an idea. Pound asked if his old friend wanted to play tennis because Ezra still dabbled in that ancient noble craft of love and deuce and break and set-point. But Eliot explained—as if Pound didn't know it already—that he did not possess an ounce of athleticism in his chemistry. Tom was an observer, not a doer of deeds on courts of tennis.

The incarcerated poet mentioned to the poet who was free that in the ancient times the ideal was not merely to be brainy, as Eliot was, but rather, like Pound himself, to be both brainy and brawny, to play sports, not so much to win, but to show the world that you were a good sport, that you were really a gentleman. No, no, no, Eliot said, he could not be classified in such a manner. He pointed out to Ezra that, after all, Tom was a halfway decent skipper on a sailboat. Didn't that count for something?

—Fair enough, Pound said.

Then he was silent.

—So what brings you to Washington and the Bughouse? he asked his old friend.

—Your case, Eliot said. There is a possibility that we can spring you at last. There are a few more hurdles, but the hardest ones have been surmounted.

—And that jew-loving Roosevelt is gone, Pound fumed. He won't have me to kick around anymore.

—We formed a committee, Tom said.

Pound answered in a dead-pan:

—That sounds promising.

Eliot explained that they were meeting for the express purpose of discussing Pound's situation at the hospital. Pound pointed out how futile their committee was because, as he said, life at St. Elizabeths was life without parole.

—The Inferno, Pound said.

—It could be worse, Eliot declared.

Pound was astonished.

How could it be worse?

—How could it be worse, Tom?

—You might never get out, whereas I am saying that we are devising a way for your release from the hospital. It could be worse because there could be no hope. What I am saying to you is that there is now reason to hope, old boy. There is reason to believe that you are going to get out.

Then Eliot, perhaps because he sensed the hope, now joked with his old friend.

—What was it Gertrude Stein called you?

—The town crier, Pound said, downbeat and less hopeful than his friend. Where did that Yid come from?

Eliot asked whom he meant.

—Fucking Stein, Pound said.

—Oakland, Eliot answered.

—Oakland?

—Where, apparently, there is no there, there.

ELIOT Where, apparently,
There is no there, there.

EP. It's clever, Possum,
But nothing more than that.
Hemingway got on his high horse
With me regarding that Yid
Stein. He said it was ugly
What I was saying about her,
I told him where to go.

ELIOT. Hemingway?

EP. I told him where to go.
He said speaking like that
Was beneath me.

ELIOT. Perhaps he boxed
Too many rounds
By then.

EP. Perhaps.
Would you like some tea?

ELIOT. You have tea?

EP. There are some amenities
Which I managed
To secure
Over the years.
Tea is one of them.

ELIOT. What kind?

EP. Earl Grey, is that all right?

ELIOT. Superb.

EP. You like it with milk, right?

ELIOT. A splash.

EP. We vill drink
To the likes
Of all the kikes,
Here and in the clink.

ELIOT. Silly man.

EP. We are old friends.
We are like Dante and Guido.

ELIOT. You were always
Il miglior fabbro.
So I guess that makes me
Guido Cavalcanti.
One could do worse.
One might be
Shakespeare.

(They laugh uproariously again)

Then Pound banged on loudly, as he boiled the water for tea, about usury. Even Eliot, who was normally quite tolerant of Pound's tirades about the Jews, found himself looking at his watch. Hurry up, please, it's time, he thought. Eliot said that war was the great curse, not so much usury, but Pound pointed out to him that war is caused by usury. They are handmaidens. They are buddies. They are bedfellows. Usury and war were like nothing else in their universe. It was the oil that drove the engine of civilization, the machines that brought prosperity to the few and misery to the many. But that was not Ezra's concern. He had an uncanny ability not to give a fig about the common man, about the masses; he and Possum often had a good laugh about that phrase, "the masses." But the Jews? The Jews were another matter, Ezra said. Oh, leave the Jews alone, Eliot said, and give me a cuppa, Ezra.

—I'll give you a cuppa, Pound said, laughing in a way that did not so much confuse Eliot as to make him at times wary of his old friend.

Ezra managed to create a card table which he had assembled into a proper table for their tea. He laid down a linen for the tablecloth, placed unmatched but lovely tea cups and plates out, and rifled around in the mess of papers and books, dragging out a bag of biscuits for them. McVitie's. Someone or other had brought them over from England. Digestives. He poured some milk into the tiny white pitcher. He found some pound cake with some fruit in it, sliced it and placed the pieces on another colorful plate. The setting actually looked beautiful, so elegant and civilized; it almost made the noise and madness which surrounded them a palatable distraction.

They sat.

The tea steeped, then Pound poured the tea into their cups.

You could see that Eliot appreciated these gestures from Pound. He seemed almost choked up, a man who rarely showed any public display of emotion.

They sipped tea and ate pound cake and nibbled on their biscuits.

The afternoon light reminded Eliot of a poem by Emily Dickinson.

It was the slant of light.

Even Eliot was tired of speaking about usury, so he said:

—There is no problem that tea cannot halve.

—But does it cohere? Pound asked.

—Coherence is over-inflated, Eliot said, dismissively. And besides which, what bloody doesn't cohere, Ezra? Is it our lives, our work, or even our tea time? Why must it cohere?

EP. Remember how baggy
"The Waste Land" was
Before I got me mitts on it?

ELIOT. It did not cohere.

EP. Until it did.

ELIOT. Then it did.

EP. Then it did.

(Pause)

ELIOT. I'm here to help.

EP. The way out
And the way in
Are often the same.

ELIOT. Here is a place of disaffection
Time before and time after
In a dim light

Out of nowhere, it would seem, Eliot began to speak about Valerie. He said that no one understood him quite like Valerie. But Ezra was having trouble figuring out who Valerie was. Did Possum mean Paul Valery? in which case, yes, Valery was someone worth talking about. But no, no, Possum was speaking about is wife Valerie, not Viv, the first wife who wound up in her own bughouse, so that Pound said to himself, careful, Ez, careful, no sense passing judgment about Possum's first wifey when he (Ez) himself was incapacitated in his own bughouse, the bughouse of all bughouses, here at St. Elizabeths. Ez used to joke with some of his more enlightened and well-educated Bughouse classmates that he was a product of the University of Pennsylvania, Hamilton College, and St. Elizabeths. A fine pedigree, one of his inmate friends confessed. But just when Ezra was beginning to open up with this fellow—his name was Stewart Coyne—and Ezra would joke with him, calling him Coyne of the Realm, and Stewart, in turn, would call Ezra, His Poundship, the Exchequer of the Loony Bin. But then Stewart hit a bad patch a while ago, Ezra hadn't seen him on the fair grounds, as he called the grounds around the buildings, and then he learned one day that Stewart had topped himself, i.e., committed hari-kari, as Pound put it, using his own sheets to affect the deed what was gone.

Eliot was saying that no one quite understood him like his wife Valerie, and then he went on, almost weepily, to say that no one understood his own poetry quite like Ezra did. Ezra joked that when the writer was ready, the editor appeared. Nonetheless, he was flattered by what Possum had to say regarding Ezra's extraordinary editorial gifts.

Back in the old days, back in the teens and twenties, there was no one quite like Ezra Pound, Eliot often said to anyone who might listen. Pound was smart and savvy, generous and compassionate, but tough as nails, and with the highest of standards, not just for himself, but for those he edited. Everyone benefited from his largesse: Eliot, Joyce, Hemingway, Frost, Ford, Lewis, et al.

> ELIOT. I am here,
> We all are here
> To help.
> You have been here
> Long enough.
> It is time.

> History may be
> Servitude,
> History may be
> Freedom.

> History now bends
> Towards freedom
> For Ezra Pound.

> EP. Like the old Jew said,
> If only, if only.

> ELIOT. The time is right.

> EP. If only…

CHAPTER NINE

"When one's friends hate each other
　how can there be peace in the world?
Their asperities diverted me in my green time."
　　　　—"Canto CXV"

It was a white-shoe law firm, the walls of their offices were a flesh color, and someone joked that it was lined with the skin of other writers. No one laughed. It was a dour lot, some lawyers (the suits) and some writers (some of the greatest of all time): T. S. Eliot, dressed almost like a lawyer himself, wearing pinstriped suit, white shirt, tie, polished brogues on his feet; William Carlos Williams, the good doctor, wearing khakis and a blue blazer, a blue buttoned-down shirt and a tie, somehow looking sporty and elegant, casual and yet professional and formal; Ernest Hemingway, wearing khaki trousers and desert boots, a white dress shirt, buttoned down, but open at the collar, several buttons down, his big chest showing, and over this he wore a beautifully crisp khaki-colored safari jacket, an expensive wrist watch on his wrist, a watch he kept looking at as if he needed to be somewhere shortly; Archibald MacLeish, the poet, former employee of the Roosevelt administration, a poet's poet, well connected and influential, a man about town, dressed in a very Ivy League suit, the padding off the shoulders, the suit seemed to form-fit his frame, and he wore a crisp white shirt and a handsome, colorful tie, and a pair of brown loafers on his feet, with argyle socks; Robert Frost, wearing an outfit that sat some-where between a farmer's Sunday dress and a poet's idea of how a writer should dress, no tie (the only one, besides Hemingway) not wearing a tie, he wore a shirt jacket over a well-ironed blue work-shirt, a pair of working boots on his feet; and James Laughlin, the publisher, Ezra Pound's publisher, and a poet himself, the person who sent mon-ey to Pound regularly, so that the incarcerated poet could have tea and biscuits, purchase books, and order office sup-plies—ribbons for his typewriter, notebooks to write in, pens and pencils, envelopes, scotch tape, staples, rulers, and some money to get clothes and whatever else Pound needed, including toothpaste and soap, a comb and brush (yes, though his hair looked like a bird's nest, Pound did comb his hair regularly), mouthwash, new socks, gloves, a hat in the cold weather. The list went on and on, James Laughlin said, of what Ezra Pound needed.

—It's time to give freedom to the poets, Hemingway said.

—Agreed, Laughlin concurred.

—The issue is how to affect this positive change for Ezra, Archibald MacLeish said.

—How to get him free and let him go on his way, Eliot added.

—Where? one of the lawyers asked.

—Italy, Eliot answered.

—But will the government agree to let him leave the country?

It was another one of the white-shoe lawyers raising an-other serious question.

—As I understand it, yes, Williams told him. The government would be more than happy to see the back of Ezra Pound.

Everyone laughed, some heartily (the writers) and some formally (the lawyers).

—It's time, Hemingway said. They need to let him go. *Basta!*

Yet a third lawyer addressed Hemingway without letting him know that the author was his favorite writer and he was as if a young boy in a room with his favorite baseball player.

—That is what we intend to do today, Mr. Hemingway.

—Good, Hemingway said. It is good.

It may have been good, but Hemingway looked nervous and impatient, again, looking at his expensive watch as if he had to be somewhere shortly.

—Good, he repeated.

—This is business, Mr. Hemingway, T. S. Eliot said, looking very much like the director of a major publishing house in London, which he had been and still was. It is nothing personal here. We have all had our run-ins with Ezra, both when we were younger and even more recently when we have visited him at St. Elizabeths.

—I frankly can't stand his poetry, Robert Frost said, looking old and sour and then around the room, trying to find someone to nod or shout Amen to his pronouncement.

—The point of this meeting is not to pass judgment on his poetry, a fourth lawyer said. The point of the meeting is to come up with a strategy for Mr. Pound's release from

St. Elizabeths. We need to present a cogent literary and legal argument to vacate the original order which put him in lock-up at the hospital in Washington. The first argument is that the penalty for his so-called crime is disproportionate to the price he is now paying. Everyone accused of treason during the Second World War has been released from prison. The only person still locked up is Ezra Pound. That's the legal argument in a nutshell.

—I have known Ezra nearly all of my adult life, Bill Williams said. We were classmates at the University of Pennsylvania. Our politics were never sympathetic to each other; our poetics are divergent too. But there comes a time when such petty matters get put aside and we conclude that the penalty is disproportionate to the crime and Ezra needs to be released from St. Elizabeths. He is neither a threat to himself nor to others. He's an old man now; he's in his seventies.

The first lawyer, the head of the firm actually, spoke up again.

—Dr. Williams' points are well taken, he said. The penalty is disproportionate. Others have been released. It is time that Ezra Pound were released too.

Eliot concurred.

—So we agree to a common goal today. A common purpose. We wish to liberate Ezra Loomis Pound from incarceration.

—Our collective wish to liberate him is greater than any superficial differences we have entertained with him in the past.

Hemingway was back on board.

—It is a good time to release poets from prisons.

—It has been a long time coming, Archibald MacLeish said.

Robert Frost had been silent. Then he spoke up in his plain-spoken way. He wanted to know whose idea was it to put Ezra Pound into St. Elizabeths in the first place. He noted that had Pound stood trial, he probably would have been released years ago.

Across from him sat James Laughlin, the publisher of New Directions, Pound's publisher and friend. Laughlin admitted that the idea was dreamed up by him and his lawyer. They had decided that a trial was too risky, he said, the consequences were too great. Treason was punishable by death, although several other people, they now learned, in similar positions to Pound's were not sentenced to death and were out of prison within a few years.

LAWYER. We did it
To protect
Mr. Pound.
It was to
Prevent him
From being
Executed.

ELIOT. Rubbish.

HEMINGWAY. Utter, unadulterated
Bullshit.

LAUGHLIN. With hindsight,
We may have been guided
Differently.

It was decided that MacLeish would

MACLEISH. I have contacts
In Washington.

ELIOT. Archie, weren't you
Some kind of undersecretary
Of state?

MACLEISH. Held several positions,
Tom. Have stayed in touch
With old friends.
    And the time is right.

ELIOT. What is it you want us
To do for Ezra Pound?

MACLEISH. We need a petition
To put together. We need to write
Letters to Congressmen and Senators
And even to the President of the
United States, asking for clemency,
Even a pardon.
It looks very bad
That one of our finest poets
Is locked away in an
Insane asylum
For twelve years.

WILLIAMS. I wrote to Harry Truman
When he was the president.
     I can draft
A letter
To Ike.
Truman said
   That he would look into
The matter.
     Maybe Ike will go farther.
I reminded Truman
    That Ezra had never
Been convicted
Of anything,
Only charged with a crime
That he never
Resolved
   In the court.
Ezra, had he been
   Convicted
Would have been out

Years ago.

Others convicted of treason
Have long ago
Been released.

ELIOT. Their convictions
Were no longer
Safe.

LAUGHLIN. Safe?

LAWYER. Mr. Eliot means that they,
That the convictions,
Were deemed
Unjust
And subsequently
    Vacated.

ELIOT. They were no longer safe.

HEMINGWAY. None of this
Explains
Why we are
Here.

Why are we
Here?

We are here
To save
Ezra Pound.

We are here
To get him out of
The Bughouse
(his words, not mine)
After 12 years,
And back
Into
The world,
A free man
Like Thomas Jefferson
Was

A free man
Like all
Poets should be.

I too hate
His politics.
But I cannot forget
The man.

We used to play
Tennis
In Paris.

ELIOT. He still plays
A lively game
At the hospital.

HEMINGWAY. We used to box.
I taught him to box.
He was a good student.
He was aggressive,
Very fit,
A good amateur athlete.

Ezra taught me
To be
Concise.

To be
Precise.

Not to waste
Words.

WILLIAMS. If only
Ez
Had not wasted
Words.

ELIOT. He was protean.
We each are indebted
To him
In our own ways.

He showed me how
An editor
Can be as creative
As the writer.

He edited my
Inchoate,
My incoherent,
Words and ideas,
My unpublishable
Work,
& he made it
Publishable.

FROST. Like everyone here,
I'm indebted to him.
He got me published
When no one would
Publish me.

But I hate his politics,
And I can't really

Tolerate the man
Either.

But there are principles.
He needs to be released.

LAUGHLIN. Because the time has come
To petition
The government
For his release.

MACLEISH. Keep in mind
That he's never been
Tried for treason.
His trial was jettisoned.
It would be all but
Impossible
To assemble Italians
Who can speak and understand
English
Two of them for every charge.

LAUGHLIN. I should have done it
Differently.
 If I had it to do over,
I would do it
Differently.

ELIOT. What's past is past.
Past is prologue.
Act One is over.
Act Two needs to close too.
The arrest. The incarceration.

WILLIAMS. We are his
Deus ex machina.

ELIOT. Indeed.
We are.

WILLIAMS. Pound gets sprung.

HEMINGWAY. Let him go back
To Italy, walk the promenade,
Finish his long poem,
Live the rest of his life
In peace—
Free.

WILLIAMS. How do you spring
Ezra Pound?

There!
It happens.

How did Ezra thank them for springing him from the Bug House? He would leave America immediately, he said. He would sail on an Italian liner for Italy. As he stood in a forward area of the ship, which was docked at Pier 90 in Hell's Kitchen, waiting to be cleared to leave the dock. It would be guided by tug boats down the North River which tourists and non-New Yorkers constantly called the Hudson River, which actually was north of the North. Ezra stood on the forward area deck, paparazzi snapping his photograph. He wore loose trousers and comfortable shoes; he had on a flowing, loose-fitting linen shirt. He looked like a poet, whatever a poet looked like. He certainly didn't look like an FBI agent or a Customs Inspector. Nor did he look quite like anyone else on the ship, including a few artsy passengers on their way for an old fashioned Grand Tour. Who knows what possessed him, but he got the bright idea to raise his hand in the Fascist salute. It would be a kind of fuck-you forever to America.

The next day, the ship already at sea, the papers were filled with his photograph, delivering the salute.

—He is a dog, an old Jewish intellectual on the Upper West Side said, as he looked at the photograph in the morning paper as he ate his breakfast in a luncheonette on Broadway at the corner of West 87th Street. This is a poet, the intellectual said, who has no compassion for anyone, who possesses no sympathy for the downtrodden. In other words, he is shit; he is a shit. He is a monster.

—Good riddance, his friend, an Irish actor said. We'll all be glad to see the back of that one.

—Six million people had to die, so that he could get out of a mental hospital to give the Fascist salute on the deck of the Italian ship. Where is the justice?

—There is no justice, a black man who worked as a busboy in the luncheonette said. He was friends with all the men eating breakfast in the luncheonette because they had been coming into the place for thirty years, as long as he had been a busboy. There is no damn justice in this world.

CHAPTER TEN

"nothing matters but the quality
of the affection—
in the end—that has carved the trace in the mind
dove sta memoria"
        —"Canto LXXVI"

It was December, cold and snowy outside, but inside Russell and Kathy's apartment, it was toasty warm and welcoming. The guests arrived one by one or in two's mostly. They had come from nearby in Brooklyn, on other streets in Park Slope, or they had come out from Manhattan, either on the subway or they drove out, across the bridge, and into this old borough, Whitman's Brooklyn. It was late in the 1980s, everyone settling down and raising families, moving into nicer apartments, taking jobs teaching at various universities. Among the guests, there was Paul and his wife Siri, there was the poet and editor Grace, by herself, and then there was Dermot and his wife, the pianist Yazuko from Japan. There were others, but Dermot didn't seem to know who they were. He knew Russell and Paul, and was getting to know the others. The evening was a celebration of one of them selling a book or getting tenure or something like that, but Dermot, being a big drinker in those days, couldn't remember what the occasion was for the dinner party. Maybe it was just social, a way to get together and celebrate their own lives. Being a writer wasn't easy at any time, but certainly in the 1980s, everything was there to say that writing was irrelevant. Reagan was president, and no one present liked him. The talk was about Iran-Contra and Oliver North, a lot of dirty dealing and back-stabbing by the politicians. Trickle-down economics had proved itself a great fraud already. If there was a future, it was the writers and their ideas. Paul was talking about Salman Rushdie, and Russell praised some poets he knew, Bill Matthews and some others he had known. Kathy spoke about her work with the Associated Writing Programs, but the writers at the dinner did not much care for organizations, except maybe New York PEN, which at least fought to get people out of prison.

Pound was dead. He died in Venice, back in the Seventies. He died after a visit to America, then instead of going home to his wife Dorothy in Rapallo, he went to Venice to be with Olga, his mistress, his true love. The Eighties were a time when all the Wild Ones, all the gifted and completely other ones took their professorships at the universities, and settled down, if they could, buying places in Brooklyn, just before everyone moved out there. Russell was just such a writer. He had moved from wherever it was he had been teaching, yes, up in New Hampshire, and then down to the city for a while, then around the country to various universities, finally settling down in Brooklyn, teaching in New Jersey.

Russell said that the weather reminded him of New England, where he was from, just north of Boston. In New England, when everyone was completely fed up with winter, it came back for one more round with everyone. It seemed to have an interminable grip on their lives. It had been such a winter.

It was April, but you would never guess it by the weather.

—Snow in April, Grace said, as if it were the title of a poem she was about to recite.

—The cruelest month, Dermot said. But none of them cared for T. S. Eliot and the remark was ignored.

—Wine? Russell asked.

—I'm all right, Siri said.

—Migraine? Kathy asked her.

—A little, Siri said.

—There is no such thing as a little migraine, Kathy said. It's either a migraine or it's something else, and if it's a migraine, it grips you and demands all your attention. The light. The sounds. Everything is against you.

—That's what it is, Siri confessed. I was under the duvet all afternoon.

—Then wine is out, Kathy said.

—But it's good to get out.

—Baseball season is upon us, Paul declared.

He was a striking looking man, dark and handsome, well spoken in English and French, well educated, a real presence. His wife Siri was beautiful, one of those tall Nordic blondes from somewhere like Minnesota, where everyone is above average and good looking in a very white way.

People said that Russell looked like Hemingway, but he only looked like Hemingway if you weren't exactly sure what Hemingway looked like. He was burly and he had a

New England accent, faintly Bostonian. His novels were hitting some high notes lately, as were Paul's, the two of them some of the best writers anywhere. Siri would have to wait a bit longer to be recognized, but her writing would take hold some years later. Russell would leave Kathy not too long after the dinner party, and marry the woman who would become his fourth—or fifth—and final wife. That would be the poet Chauncey Snow; but that was somewhere down the road, and this dinner party was very much of its moment, as if nothing existed but the people in that pleasant, well furnished Brooklyn room.

Paul asked Dermot what he thought of the Mets and Dermot confessed that he had never been into baseball.

—That's sacrilege, Paul laughed.

Siri said: Paul sees baseball

The way other people

See religion.

There's the ritual,

But also there is

The belief,

The system itself

As its own

Universe.

Russell said that he was not going to think about the Red Sox until later in the season.

—Let them stew in their own mediocrity, he said.

—The curse of the Bambino, Pal said.

DERMOT. I said that to Russell's friend
Bill up in Boston,
    And he practically tore me
A new asshole.

RUSSELL. You New Yorkers,
He probably said. You never let go
Of that Bambino story.

PAUL. Guilty as charged.

DERMOT. That's exactly what he said.

RUSSELL. We haven't won
A World Series
  In nearly 70 years.

PAUL. Not this year either.
The Yankees are ferocious,
Even though I hate them.

RUSSELL. No, it doesn't look good
For the Red Sox.

GRACE. Can't we talk about
Anything
  Other than sports?

KATHY. Would you like some wine, Grace?

GRACE. A little.
You know the Jews.

We are not much
For drinking.

KATHY. I'm not much
Of a drinker either.
But a little wine
At a party
And with the meal...

Siri asked for water and Kathy said that she had found a bottle of Evian at a nearby bodega, but not just any bottle of Evian. It was a glass bottle, she said.

—I spoke to Rushdie today, Paul said.

Rushdie was in hiding after the fatwa was given. His story had become a life on the run.

RUSSELL. How is he?

PAUL. He's still in hiding.

GRACE. The Muslims are insufferable
With their *fatwas* against writers.

PAUL. Israel is no saint.

GRACE. I'm not saying they are.
But they have a right to protect
Themselves against the depredations
Of the Muslim world.

DERMOT. This is turning
Into

A real New York
Dinner party.

KATHY. Is everyone all right
With fish?

RUSSELL. I poached a whole salmon.

KATHY. There are lots of other things too.

RUSSELL. Let's all sit down.
I'll open some white wine
For the fish.

PAUL. It's Brooklyn,
And yet none of us is from
Brooklyn.

GRACE. I grew up in Brooklyn.
Out in Flatbush.

DERMOT. I also grew up in Brooklyn.

SIRI. I thought you were Irish.

DERMOT. I am Irish,
But I also grew up
In Brooklyn,
And even though I was not born
Here
Nor did I go to high school here,
Fifteen
Of my siblings

Were born
    In St. Mary's Hospital
In Bedford-Stuyvesant.
St. Mary's is Al Sharpton's
Headquarters these days.
It's off Eastern Parkway.

KATHY. I thought you were Jewish.

GRACE. You can be Irish and Jewish, Kathy.

PAUL. Leopold Bloom.

KATHY. I'm definitely not from Brooklyn.

RUSSELL. Nor I.
But I do love it here.

SIRI. I'm from Minnesota.
Anyone else from Minnesota.
No. I thought so.

PAUL. Joizy, me.

GRACE. (To Dermot) I guess we'll have to show
Them what people from Brooklyn
Are like,
    Hey,
Dermot?

DERMOT. (Affecting tough-guy voice) You talkin' to
me?

GRACE. (Toughly) Yeah, I'm talkin' to you.

DERMOT. Do you know how people
In Brooklyn greet each other?

RUSSELL. Tell us.

GRACE. How ya doin'?

DERMOT. And the response?

KATHY. Tell us.

DERMOT. How ya doin' or how are *you* doin'?

RUSSELL. Let's eat.

KATHY. More wine for anyone?

PAUL. Me.

GRACE. I'm starting a new reading series
At the Y. It's going to be
Contemporary writers
Speaking about an older generation
Of writers.

SIRI. I know who Paul would speak on.

KATHY. Someone French.

SIRI. No.

GRACE. William Carlos Williams.

SIRI. Guess again.

GRACE. Frank O'Hara.

SIRI. Colder, but not cold.

RUSSELL. Charles Olson.

SIRI. Warmer.

RUSSELL. Robert Creeley.

SIRI. Warmer.

DERMOT. Ezra Pound.

SIRI. Bingo!

KATHY. Ezra Pound?

PAUL. With reservations
And caveats.

GRACE. I detest Ezra Pound,
And I certainly wouldn't let anyone
Speak about him
At the Y,
With its long Jewish tradition.

PAUL. It is because of his politics
And his wrong-headed ideas,

That the Y should entertain a talk
About him.
     His influence as a poet
Is immense.
      So is his influence
As an editor—
As a taste-shaper.

As a spirit.
     His energy.

  His vitality.

GRACE. He's an anti-Semite, Paul.
And you're Jewish.

PAUL. His friends were Jewish.
The Objectivists were practically all Jewish.
Oppen, Zukofsky, Reznikoff, etc.

GRACE. Pound was a virulent propagandist
For the Italian Fascists. He was wholly
Complicit in the arrest and execution
Of the Jews,
     Both in Germany and Italy.

PAUL. You're not looking at the poetry.

GRACE. I am looking at the poetry.
His crude anti-Semitism is found
Everywhere throughout that abomination
Known as *The Cantos*,
The most overrated

Piece of incoherent
Crap
That ever was
Written
 Or
     Published.

PAUL. He paid for his radio speeches
During the war. He spent
Twelve years
          Incarcerated
        At St. Elizabeths
In Washington.

GRACE. We can never forgive him.
We must never forgive him.
He was part of the Axis that killed
Six million Jews. We will never forget.

PAUL. Ezra Pound was a poet.
He didn't kill any Jews.

GRACE. You don't know what
You are talking about, Paul.

PAUL. You've closed off your mind to him.

GRACE. (Standing) I'm leaving.

KATHY. Don't go, Grace.

RUSSELL. It's snowing terribly
Outside. You can't leave now.

PAUL. Opening day.

GRACE. Where's my coat, Kathy.

KATHY. Oh, Grace, please,
Please,
Don't go out into that storm.

GRACE. It is not possible
For me
To stay,
Kathy.

RUSSELL. If you have to go,
At least let me walk you
To the subway station.

KATHY. Or let us call you a cab.

GRACE. That's all right.
I'm the Brooklyn native.
I'll take the subway.
I'm from Flatbush.
Park Slope is not exactly
Dangerous territory.

RUSSELL. Let me walk you there.
I'll get my coat.

GRACE. That's all right, Russell.
Thank you.

RUSSELL. It's no problem, Grace.

GRACE. Stay with your guests.

(Grace leaves)

PAUL. If she only read his poems—

SIRI. Let it be, Paul.

RUSSELL. Where were we?

KATHY. More wine.

DERMOT. Now I'm the last one
From Brooklyn. (To Paul)
Did I ever tell you
About my Ezra Pound story?

RUSSELL. Tell us.

PAUL. More wine.

KATHY. Yes, more wine.

DERMOT. I was walking down West 4th Street…

PAUL. Positively West 4th Street.

SIRI. Dylan was writing that song
About 4th Street in Minneapolis.

DERMOT. This was in the Village
One evening, and I see this fellow in the
Doorway of Sevilla, the Spanish
Restaurant at West 4th and Charles.
He looks just like Ezra Pound,
And I'm drunk, so I go over to him.
He's with a few other people,
Very old and very frail, he was.
"Are you *il miglior fabbro*?" I ask.
Si, si, si, he says, *"Io sono."*

(Pause)

Paul Blackburn had told a bunch of us
That in order to get to see Pound
In Rapallo or Venice, Olga Rudge
Made you recite one of his poems.
So I said to the man in the doorway
Of the Sevilla restaurant:

"Bah! I have sung women in three cities,
But it is all the same;
And I will sing of the sun."
He smiled,
and then
They went on their way and I went
Back on my way
towards the Lion's Head
Or wherever it was I was going that night.

That was not even twenty years ago.
But Paul is right. It is finally only
The poetry that counts, not the man,

Not his politics, not even his actions.
Only the poems. Thirty or forty years
From now people will see that Paul
Was right. Only the poetry matters.
All the rest is dross.

KATHY. More wine?

RUSSELL. Let's have some dessert.

PAUL. Opening day and it's snowing.

KATHY. Some water, Siri?

SIRI. Yes, more water. (Pause)
Has anyone seen the new Modernist
Show at the Met?

RUSSELL. Which one?

SIRI. It just opened last week.

PAUL. It's worth getting there
To see. Go early.

SIRI. Stay late.

KATHY. We're going to the Guston show.

RUSSELL. Next week.

SIRI. Do you think Grace is all right?

PAUL. Grace will be fine.
She's a tough cookie.

RUSSELL. I could go look for her.

KATHY. Stay.

(Pause)

DERMOT. I'm the last person from Brooklyn.

PAUL. You and several million others.

DERMOT. No, in this room. Here.
In this apartment. Tonight.
I'm the last one, and
I sense Ezra Pound here.

PAUL. To *il miglior fabbro*!

RUSSELL. May his poems live forever!

ALL. To his poems.

(Glasses clink)

CHAPTER ELEVEN

"I sat on the Dogana's steps
For the gondolas cost too much, that year,
And there were not 'those girls,' there was one face,
And the Buccentoro twenty yards off, howling 'Stretti,'
The lit cross-beams, that year, in the Morosini,
And peacocks in Koré's house, or there may have been."
　　—"Canto III"

1.

Her rooms in Venice overlooked the canal. The windows were opened. The smell of the sea wafted into the room. It was the autumn; the tourists had fled, along with summer. As evening approached, there was a hint of the winter in the air. Boats went past the windows. Olga sat in her study along with the poet Allen Ginsberg, who had come to visit Pound. Olga usually had visitors recite something from Pound's work before she granted a visit with him. But she already knew Allen; he did not need to be tested on his knowledge of Ezra Pound or any other poet. Allen was the real deal, as far as Olga was concerned, and she knew that Ezra liked him, was even looking forward to the visit. The end was nigh, Ezra joked with Olga that morning, as he coughed and coughed, his reedy body shaking as he did so. But the end was near, and she knew it, and so did Ezra. Death was not something he feared; his fears were caught up in *The Cantos*, that he did not write everything he intended to write, and also his profound belief that the work did not cohere, and that he had not done it correctly. It was 1970, and he was nearly 85 years old; his birthday was October 30th, in a few weeks. Would he even make it? But he seemed to prevail, getting through the sticky, humid summer, and now the back of one season had broken over the head of another. Autumn was in the air. Sing! Sing! Goddamn! Then these words came into his head, as if for the first time: *The ant's a centaur in his dragon world.* Pull down your vanity, Ez. It is not man made courage, or made order, or made grace. Learn of the green world what can be your place in scaled invention or true artistry. Pull down your vanity, Old Ezra.

2.

Olga suddenly changed her mind and said:

—The rule is that if you can't recite one of his poems, Olga said, you can't get in.

Allen did not just recite a poem, he sang it.

So that the vines burst from my fingers
And the bees weighted with pollen
Move heavily in the vine-shoots:
chirr – chirr – chir-rikk – a purring sound,
And the birds sleepily in the branches.

—Very well, Mr. Ginsberg.
—Allen, he said.

—You may call me Miss Rudge. We are all Americans, and yet so many years living abroad, I might as well be from Venice.

—It was the top of "Canto XVII" I sang, Allen told her.

—I know which bloody canto you were reciting, Mr. Ginsberg. I wasn't born yesterday.

—So will he see me today?

She looked out the window.

Paused. Thought.

—We'll see, she said. I don't want to get your hopes up. He is not well. He's frailer than ever.

—It is most important to speak with him, Allen said. And I know half the *Cantos*, all of *Cathay*, *Personae*, all the prose books, the early poems, the later ones. *Pisan Cantos*. I grew up on Pound. William Carlos Williams was my family doctor; he delivered me.

—Really?

—Really and truly, and he wrote the introduction to *Howl*. Me and Doc Williams go way back.

—Ezra and Bill did not always get along. But they were lifelong friends. Bill was critical and Ezra was sometimes dismissive. He thought Bill was a provincial, and proud of it. In many respects, Bill Williams was Ezra's favorite mutt. He was devastated when Bill died ten years ago.

—In '63.

—Yes, seven years ago. Ezra was distraught over Bill's death.

GINSBERG. "Epitaphs"
Fu I
Fu I loved the high cloud and the hill,
Alas, he died of alcohol.

Li Po
And Li Po also died drunk.
He tried to embrace a moon
In the Yellow River.

—*Entre, prego*, Olga said.

—*Grazie mille.*

—What brings you to Venice, Mr. Ginsberg?

—I've come to see the Old Master.

As if on cue, Ezra Pound enters the room, wearing a flowing and light colored shirt and trousers, with leather sandals on his feet, his hair long and swept back, his skin as wrinkled as W. H. Auden's.

—Do you want tea? she asked the Old Master.

—Tea, he said.

He sat down next to Allen Ginsberg. He smiled. Allen bowed in an overly dramatic way. He shouted: *Il miglior fabbro*. And Pound said: Well, that was Dante, not me. But Eliot thought otherwise. He would, wouldn't he? I edited "The Waste Land" for him.

Before Olga left the room to get them some tea, she told Allen, as if Ezra were not there: He sometimes lapses into long silences. He sometimes chooses not to speak at all.

—I understand, Allen told her. I have studied with zen masters who believed that silence was the only way.

Olga did not seem to hear Ginsberg's remark. She said:

—Then again he may wish to speak a lot. I don't know his moods well enough to advise you about where he is today.

As she left the room, Allen saw that Pound's lips were moving, though nothing seemed to be coming out, word-wise. Ginsberg stood next to the Old Master and tried to discern whether anything was being said. Allen had his pen and notebook to hand. Be there when it happens, he thought. Write it down.

Pound continued to mumble.

He was sat in a hard-back chair, and Allen took a seat in a similar chair facing Pound.

—I have tried to write Paradise, Pound finally said.

—You did, Ginsberg told him.

—But I failed, Pound told him.

4.

The light was blue and pearly, late afternoon light, and Venetian light, a kind of light of light. A breeze wafted into the room from the canal outside the window. Birds could be heard singing nearby. Allen wondered what kind of birds they were.

EP. The life. The work.
How I treat others.
But mostly the life.

(Pause)

The work.

(Pause)

It does not cohere.
I know nothing.
I am a blank canvas.
I am a cipher.
Zed. Zero. Nada.
Niente.
Nothing.

GINSBERG. The poem,
Your poem,
The Cantos,
Is the great 20th century
Poem of image,
Object directly treated,
News that stays news,
The rhythm of action,
The rhythm of experience,
All this was yours,
Was your invention.

EP. Nothing.

5.

AG. Nothing?
EP. Nothing.
AG. Why?
EP. Why, what?
AG. Nothing.
EP. I don't know.
AG. You don't know.
EP. Yes.
AG. Why?
EP. Why?
AG. Yes.
EP. Because.
AG. That's an answer?
EP. Yes.

(**Pause**)

I am a foolish old man.
I have hurt too many people.
I am not who they think I am.
I am not a good man.
I am not even a good poet.
I have failed on every front.
I am an empty coat.
I am a bag of old bones.

I thought I knew a thing or two.
I thought.
Then I realized that I knew
Nothing.
They are words w/out meaning.
They are empty.

6.

GINSBERG. It is the empty mirror.
It's very zen, Ole Ez, it's the conundrum
That life is everything and is nothing,
And yet something happens.
There!

(Pause)

Hey, did you dig the records I bought you?
The Bob Dylan. Donovan. The Beatles.

EP. I did.

GINSBERG. Let me sing to you.
Oh, sunflower, weary of time…

EP. That's all right.
That's fine.
Let it be.

GINSBERG. How about I chant:
Hare Krishna
Hare Krishna
Krishna Krishna
Hare Hare
Hare Rama
Rama Rama
Hare Hare

EP. I like the chant.

GINSBERG. Secret to the universe,
Uncle Ez. It could be the theme song
For the Ezuversity.

EP. The Ezuversity shuttered long ago.

(Silence)

7.

Ginsberg tried to speak about Pound's influence on American poetry, his influence upon the poets. But Ezra thought that Allen was exaggerating. From Crane to Williams, Allen said, warming up. Your influence is everywhere. At the mention of Williams, Pound laughed. Bill was his old friend, his lifelong buddy, even though they could hardly agree on anything, including where to break the line, what to write the poem about, who to address it to. Now Allen was on a roll, mentioning Kerouac and Creeley, Zukofsky and Oppen and Reznikoff. Ashbery and O'Hara, the Beats. San Francisco Renaissance. These names had the force of a freight train rolling through, at least they did for Allen Ginsberg. Pound seemed to stare off, out the window, not at Venice, but into something far beyond where they were sat. He no longer heard what Allen Ginsberg said, and these words flitted through his mind: Speak against unconscious oppression, speak against the tyranny of the unimaginative, speak against bonds. Now Ezra was back in the room in Venice and Allen Ginsberg sat across from him. When did he arrive? How did he get inside the house?

The freight train of Allen's mind chugged on, and he talked about Black Mountain and Olson, Tu Fu and Pound.

—Vanity, Pound said.

But he did not explain what he meant by the word.

—Poetry, Allen called it.

—Tear it down, Pound said.

—Kick out the jams! Allen shouted.

Yet it was not Whitman that Pound wanted to talk about, but Pound himself. Whitman was the cursed progenitor to Pound.

—Now we will argue about the sun, Ginsberg said, alluding to the Troubadours.

—Let us argue about the sun, Pound said, chuckling.

8.

GINSBERG. There are places in *The Cantos*.
Things. The poem as object,
Like the Objectivists said.

EP. No ideas but in things,
Bill Williams liked to say.

GINSBERG. Dr. Williams delivered me, Uncle Ez.

EP. Figuratively speaking.

GINSBERG. Literally.

EP. Explain.

GINSBERG. He was me mutta's obstinate
Obstetrician. His forceps squeezed me
Out of womb.

EP. Into this tomb.

GINSBERG. Into Paterson, New Joizy
Where mam and the da lived.
Dad was a poet.

EP. A foolish occupation.

GINSBERG. Didn't James Joyce
Tell you that the poets
Were the kings
  In ancient Ireland?

EP. He did.

GINSBERG. We are still kings.

EP. Deposed.

GINSBERG. Kings and queens.
I am the queen of poetry
On the Lower East Side
The East Village
Of downtown Manhattan
In New York City.
You are King Ezra!

EP. *Mozel tov!*

(Pause)

9.

—Your poems—

—My poems? Pound asked.

—Your poems—

Ginsberg searched for the words in his head and how to get them out on the tip of his tongue so that they could plunge into the liquidness of the Venetian room.

Outside the windows, gondolas glided past, motorboats sputtered along, a vaporetto put-putted by.

The word, the word, Allen thought.

He was bearded, hirsute, his hair a wild tangle of dark tendrils.

Pound was similarly made: white-bearded, his long gray hair falling every which way.

But Pound was old—as old as the lagoon, it seemed—and Ginsberg still had his youth, more or less.

Allen was middleaged; Ezra was an old man.

Pound was frail and easily tired; Ginsberg was a ball of energy.

Being in the presence of Pound, though not for the first time, was exciting to Ginsberg. He was thrilled to be having this conversation with the old bard.

Allen explained that Ezra was one of his fathers.

—Poesy goes through *Cathay* and *The Cantos*, he said.

10.

Pound made a sound somewhere between a cough and a laugh.

Here is how Allen put it:

(Pause)

About specific perceptions,
About Williams' no ideas but in things,
About direct treatment of the object—
About *le mot juste*…

EP. Flaubert.

GINSBERG. About the phrasing
Of your poems,
  About how they break
Upon the page…

EP. Once all the rage,
Now gone,
All vanity.

GINSBERG. Your poems—

EP. A way of life disappears,
The regrets remain.

Les moeurs passent, et la douleur reste.

Nothing matters but the quality
Of the affection—

In the end—
That has carved
   The trace in the mind

Dove sta memoria...

GINSBERG. The poems—
Their concrete value
For me
For others...

EP. But the poems
Make
No sense.

I tried, but failed.

GINSBERG. Tching wrote it
On his bathtub—
MAKE IT NEW!

EP. A lot of double talk,
And for me
Regarding others—
A lot of double crossing.

GINSBERG. Says who?
Cried the owl.

EP. Bunting.

GINSBERG. Basil Bunting
Says

That there is
Double-talk
In *The Cantos*?

EP. In a manner of speaking.

GINSBERG. What manner?

EP. Too little presentation,
Bunting said.
Too much reference.
Too much reference.

GINSBERG. Bunting told me,
"*The Cantos* are a model,
A model
Of economy
In the presentation
Of sensory phenomena
Via words,
     Via words—"

EP. Basil said that?

GINSBERG. He sd *The Cantos*
Are the ground
That we all walk on.

EP. A mess.

GINSBERG. You. *The Cantos*. Or me.
Or do you mean Venice itself,
Stinking and rotting from within,

Venice the cloaca of Italy,
Venice the invention of burghers,
Venice the old whore gone
Toothless in the mouth?

EP. The writing.
The writing, Ginsberg.
The writing is a mess.

(Pause)

Stupidity. Ignorance.
All the way through.
Stupidity. Ignorance.

11.

Ginsberg referred to Olson, hoping it might jar open some old chamber of Pound's memory palace and let the old poet spring to life. Allen mentioned this formula from Charles' writings:

the HEAD, by way of the EAR, to the SYLLABLE
the HEART, by way of the BREATH, to the LINE

Pound quoted from Hamlet, saying: Words, words, words.

—You never wrote a bad line, Ginsberg shouted.

But Pound countered it:

—It's hard for me to take that remark seriously. It's hard for me to write at all.

Then Allen tried to tell the old poet about their mutual friend William Carlos Williams.

—Back in 1961—Bill Williams said to me—We were talking about prosody, I asked him to explain your prosody, and Williams said: Pound has a mystical ear. Did Dr. Williams ever tell you that?

—No, he did not, Pound whispered.

12.

Olga said it was time for him to rest. But Ezra said he was all right, he was fine. Pound sat and stared out the window. Ginsberg sat beside him in an old wooden chair, the same as the one Pound sat in. They looked to be chairs from another century, simple and plain, and yet Venetian and elegant. The room was quite empty, only a print on one wall, seeming to be something modern and by one of Ezra's Parisian friends.

—Well, I am reporting back to you, Uncle Ezra. Bill Williams was the tender-hearted,

The tender-eyed doctor,

And that is what he said.

—We were friends, Pound told Ginsberg about his friend Bill Williams, the poet and doctor.

The baby doctor: pediatrician.

We knew each other all our lives.

We argued.

We cd not agree on much of anything.

(Silence)

But the intentions were never good.
My intentions were bad.
Everything was by accident.

Olga decided to put her foot down. Allen could see that she was about to end the interview. Ezra was tired.

—He needs his rest, she told Allen, nodding towards her ancient, wrinkled, bent,

whispering, raspy, dying partner, that human vessel of knowledge, the poet himself, the afterlife of a living legend.

—Shall I go? Ginsberg asked Ms. Rudge.

—No, stay.

As they spoke Pound was muttering to himself.

(Pause)

13.

EP. It was all by accident. An accident.
Do you understand? I had nothing
To do with any of it. It was an accident.
Spoiled by intentions. Spoiled by me.
My preoccupations: irrelevant
And stupid things. Do you know
My worst mistake, Mr. Ginsberg?

GINSBERG. Tell me, Prospero.

EP. The worst mistake I made
Was that stupid suburban prejudice,
My anti-Semitism.
That spoiled everything.

14.

The silence of the Venetian room enveloped Ezra Pound.
It was like a boa wrapping itself around the ancient one.
Olga was alarmed. Suddenly she became Gepetto protecting the human Pinocchio turning back to wood.

Pound said it again.

—That stupid suburban prejudice of anti-Semitism.

He pronounced the last word differently than he did the first time, though; in the first instance, he had a kind of caesura between the *anti* and the *Semitism*. Now he pronounced the five syllables as if it were one word, one idea, one corrosive malediction of the spirit.

He was a fool, in other words, a deeply tragic one, and his recognition scene was taking place in his beloved Venice, in front of this Jewish American poet, this beatnik-hippie, this oddball delivery of his old friend Dr. Williams.

15.

OLGA. He really must rest, Mr. Ginsberg.

GINSBERG. It is lovely
To hear you
Say that.

303

EP. Anyone could see how stupid it was.
How stupid I was.

(Pause)

Hamlet was right:
The rest is silence

It does not cohere
It does not cohere

OLGA. The tea is ready.
Let me get it. Then:
It is time to rest.
He is tired.
You will have to go, Mr. Ginsberg.

EP. It does not cohere.

(Pause)

What is the use of talking—

AG. And there is no end of talking…

EP. There is no end of things in the heart.

OLGA. *The Cantos.*

AG. Cathay.

EP. "Exile's Letter." Rihaku.

Chapter Twelve

"Time, space,
neither life nor death is the answer.
And of man seeking good,
doing evil.
In meiner Heimat
    where the dead walked
and the living were made of cardboard."
    —"Canto CXV"

The thin marble walls of the Bienecke Rare Book Library at Yale University looked almost like human skin. The light through the thin skin of marble came into the room in a peachy, fleshy color. Translucent, he thought, and it was. The place was extraordinary, by any standards. Dermot was at the Drama School, but he would not last much longer. He was drinking a bit too much. All his younger life he had said that, like John O'Hara, he wanted to go to Yale University. There were not opportunities for such a journey when he was an undergraduate—too poor, his grades good but not great, and his ability to play basketball might be good enough to make the team, but not good enough to earn a scholarship, and coming from a large, poor family, his chances of going to Yale were slim to none. But for graduate school, it was another matter. He had written his way into the school, his dialogue, they said, pitch perfect. But he had other things on his mind, other than writing a play. The dean had already spoken to him. He had said: If you don't get your act together, Dermot, you're going to be asked to leave. We like your work, when you do it, but you are here to write plays, not poetry or novels. We don't see you writing nearly enough dialogue. Is something wrong?

—I'm all right, Dermot said.

But saying he was all right was a misnomer because he was not all right.

His drinking had become exponential since coming to New Haven, and his drinking had never been anything but problematic in the past.

He told the dean that he had an idea for a play about Ezra Pound.

The dean was Jewish and didn't think this was a very good idea.

—He was a Fascist, the dean said. He was virulently anti-Semitic.

—That's the point of the play, Dermot said.

The dean thought about it.

—All right, all right, he said. I've tried to light a fire under your ass many times and have gotten nowhere fast. Maybe you'll come up with something here.

So that's how Dermot wound up at the Bienecke Library. He was given one last chance before they booted his ass out of Yale. And he had spent a good part of his young life fantasizing of going to this university. Of course, the fantasy involved his being an undergraduate there, not a graduate student. Instead he had gone to the City College. But he had gotten into Yale on the basis of his dialogue and other writings, so maybe this play about Ezra Pound might be the ticket.

The appointment with the rare book librarian was for ten o'clock in the morning and Dermot was there five minutes before the appointment.

Ezra Pound's papers—or at least a good amount of them—were housed here. Pound had died earlier in the decade. His wife Dorothy had donated his papers to the library. Dermot thought that if he could peruse these papers, he might glean a way forward with his life, writing about a poet whose work he loved but whose politics Dermot detested.

The librarian sat at one of the tables in the library and Dermot sat down opposite him.

—I understand that you wish to read in the Pound collection at the Bienecke.

—Yes, Dermot said.

—Tell me about your project.

—It's creative, not academic. But I am a grad student here. At the School of Drama. I'm in playwriting.

—I see, the librarian said. This is a research library.

—Yes, yes, there is research, Dermot assured him. That is why I wish to use the collection. I would like to read broadly, like a magpie, in the Ezra Pound collection.

The librarian was firm with him.

—We tend only to give approval to scholars, people doing doctorates or others writing books about Ezra Pound. Those sorts of projects.

—I'm writing a play. I wish to write a play about Ezra Pound's life.

—I see, the librarian said.

—My affiliation with the university, Dermot explained, is by way of the Drama School.

The librarian said it was somewhat unorthodox to allow a creative writing student use of the Pound collection. But then he added:

—But I would not say it is impossible for you to access the collection. Still, there are certain hurdles that must be jumped in order for you to read his papers.

—I understand, said Dermot.

—That you are already affiliated with the university is not necessarily a guarantee of admission to the rare book library, and yet I would think that it does not necessarily eliminate you from consideration.

Dermot had the sinking feeling that he was going to be shot down.

But then the librarian came back to him with:

—Here is what I propose that we do. I will broach the subject with Princess Mary de Rachewitz. Are you familiar with who she is?

Dermot said that he had heard the name, but he actually had not really heard it before.

—She is Ezra Pound's daughter, and she approves everyone who wishes entry into the archive.

—I see, said Dermot, sounding skeptical and a bit like the librarian.

—I will propose your idea to her and see what she says. I would imagine that she would want to speak with you personally, to find out your intentions.

Dermot paused to think of a response.

—When might this take place? he asked.

The librarian said that Princess Mary often spent time in New Haven, during various months of the year. The rest of the year she lived in a castle in northern Italy.

—Fortunately, she is resident in New Haven right now. In fact, she's in the library today on other business.

The librarian stood to leave.

—If you wait here, the librarian told Dermot, I will show her in to see you.

As the librarian walked off, Dermot tried to think of various words and lines from Ezra Pound's work. Perhaps she would want him, like Olga Rudge supposedly did, to recite some of the master's poems in order to gain entry into his world.

These thoughts were quickly stored away because Mary de Rachewitz walked into the room and over to the table where Dermot was seated. He did not think that she looked particularly like a princess; but then again he had no idea what a princess looked like. Were they all supposed to look like Grace Kelly? She sat without introducing herself. She sat there without saying anything. The room was silent. The light from the thin marble walls poured into the room in a pink glory of sunshine. Finally she spoke:

—Pro or con? she asked.

Pro or con?

Dermot did not understand the question.

He let it roll around his mind.

Pro or con?

What could the princess possibly mean?

He loved Pound's poetry; he thought the man was flawed, even tragic. Did his thinking that Pound was a tragic figure make Dermot pro or con Ezra Pound? She might take offense that Dermot considered Pound an anti-Semitic bigot, but also a literary genius. Some people wasted their youths running around from bar to bar, drinking and using drugs and chasing women or other men. Dermot wasted his youth arguing with other young poets about Ezra Pound and William Carlos Williams. They even had fist fights in places like Max's Kansas City on Park Avenue South near 17th Street, and the St. Adrian Company bar, on Broadway near Great Jones and Bleecker streets. He had scraped together pennies to buy various Ezra Pound books when he was a teenager and still remembered, broke, hungry, not having eaten in several days, selling his copy of Pound's letters to Louis Untermeyer called EP to LU. It still broke his heart that he had to sell that book in order to eat.

He said:

I am not sure

What

You mean.

Princess Mary stared at him intently. It felt like minutes passed, but maybe it was only a few seconds. Dermot sweated. He wracked his brain to come up with a response. Then it finally dawned on him what she was asking. Of course the answer was as simple as yes or no, as simple as rain or sunshine in the morning. It was part of the natural order of things, the way it was, the way it would be. *Sem-*

pre, he thought. Pro or con? The answer was right there on the tip of his tongue; all he had to do was locate it and set it free. It was a question of *breath* and *syllable*, just as the poet Charles Olson had said. It was right there like the direct treatment of the object, what Pound had said fifty years earlier. It was the rhythm of experience, the answer, the only measure that could be taken to evaluate the question and its answer. The response was as simple as pencils and erasers, sheets of lined paper, notebooks, the paraphernalia of the poet, the gear of the scholar, the playwright's friends.

He smiled.

—Pro, he said.

Mary stood to leave.

She looked down at Dermot Froidveaux, not breaking a smile or saying anything other than one word.

—Approved, she uttered.

Then she walked off and out of the room.

And he never saw her again.

M. G. STEPHENS has published 25 books, including the novels *Season at Coole* and *The Brooklyn Book of the Dead*. Two thousand-twenty-two is the 50th anniversary of the publication of *Season at Coole* by E. P. Dutton. Last year (2021), MadHat Press published his hybrid work of prose and poetry about an out of work actor who lands the part of Hamlet, and is entitled *History of Theatre or the Glass of Fashion*; it has been praised by novelists such as Hilma Wolitzer and Richard Price, as well as poets such as George Szirtes and Michael Anania. His nonfiction books include the travel memoir *Lost in Seoul* (Random House, 1990) and the essay collection *Green Dreams*, which won the AWP award in nonfiction, and was later picked by Joyce Carol Oates as one of the 100 most important American nonfiction books of the 20th century. His play *Our Father* ran on Theatre Row (42nd Street in New York) for over five years, and has had multiple productions in London, Chicago and Los Angeles. In 2001, Stephens moved abroad to London, where he lived for fifteen years. During that time he was active in London stages, and had plays produced by Pentameters Theatre in North London (Hampstead) and the Bread & Roses Theatre in South London (Clapham). He earned all his degrees after he was thirty years old, including a doctorate from the University of Essex in Colchester, England that he was awarded at the age of 60. Before moving abroad, Stephens taught creative writing workshops at Princeton, New York and Columbia universities; in London, he taught at the University of London (Queen Mary). Along with his novel *King Ezra,* Spuyten Duyvil recently published Stephens' third Coole family novel, *Kid Coole*, about a young, up-and-coming lightweight boxer out of the Hudson Valley in New York. *Season at Coole*, *The Brooklyn Book of the Dead* and *Kid Coole* comprise *The Coole Trilogy.*

Made in United States
North Haven, CT
25 June 2024

54042514R00189